The Rebel Christian Publishing

Copyright © 2024 A. Bean

ISBN: 978-1-957290-60-7 (eBook)
Print: 978-1-957290-61-4

This is a work of fiction. Any references to historical events, real people, or real places are used fictitiously. Names, characters, and places are products of the author's imagination. Inclusion of or reference to any Christian elements or themes are used in a fictitious manner and are not meant to be perceived or interpreted as an act of disrespect against such a wonderful and beautiful belief system.

Cover designed by Valicity Elaine

The Rebel Christian Publishing LLC
350 Northern Blvd STE 324 - 1390
Albany, NY 12204-1000

Visit us: http://www.therebelchristian.com/
Email us: rebel@therebelchristian.com

Contents

Bell of The Native

A Christian Fantasy Romance

By A. Bean

A Rebel Christian Publishing Book

1

Dontaye

I stare at my computer screen, burning eyes and exhaustion weighing me down. Anxiety makes my heart double thump as I try to stay focused, determined to finish what I started, but I can't fight the heavy sluggishness that tugs me back to my chair.

I pull my black frames from my tired eyes with a huff. "I give up." The words are three stabs to my heart, but I suffer the pain with a lazy sigh and sink against the seat. Without even glancing in a mirror, I know my eyes are bloodshot, so I rub the heels of my palms into them for a massage. It doesn't help.

I have no choice but to call it quits. I'm in over my head with this assignment, and I haven't even finished packing for my two-week trip to Japan. I leave in less than forty-eight hours which makes my heart double thump again, but again, I ignore it. I've been traveling the world since getting accepted into my doctorate program. Throughout all those countries, exploring so many cultures and different ways of life, I've been researching, connecting the dots, trying to find evidence to support the question of my dissertation.

Would the world be a better place without religion?

The thought of a world without religion always triggers memories of my mother. Even now, as I blink my burning, burry eyes, I try not to look at the frame sitting face down on my desk, but I betray myself and stare at it anyway. The heat of relentless anger pours into me. I hated that woman, but I couldn't get myself to get rid of the single picture that survived the fire. She was as reckless as the God she served.

Taking a breath, I let every bad thought of my mother go on the exhale. Instead of packing like a responsible human, I snatch my phone up and hit the call button. The only person who would ever answer this late is Ezra Fridman because he's a Christian and thus believes in being there for me. I've told him I'm not interested in his religion and even told him I'd mention him in my paper about how pushy Christians can be. I thought this would make him calm down a little, if not at least take the hint that I was not interested in his faith, but it had the opposite effect entirely. Ezra felt proud—honored was the word he actually used. He even told me that citing him meant I'd get to cite all the scriptures he's used in our conversations and that would change me. I seriously doubt it.

"Hello?" Ezra answers.

Groggy and tired, his voice forces a smile to my face.

"Ezra, wake up. I'm hungry."

"Why do you need me if you're *hungry*?"

"Do you really want your precious friend to be out at two in the morning all alone?" I listen for his answer with a small smile. He sighs and I know he'll give in. He always sighs instead of fights because he knows he can't tell me 'No.'

"Fine, I'll be there in ten. But I'm not coming up."

"I'll be waiting by the door."

I hang up without saying 'bye' and race for the bathroom to freshen up. I ruffle my curls, twisting and tying them until I get them into a thick bun atop my head. With skin the color of honey, I've only got to pinch my cheeks to get a natural blush. I don't want to look like I'm trying too hard. Or trying at all, but who am I kidding?

I can admit that Ezra is attractive. He doesn't look like any Christian boy I've ever seen. You know, the nerdy, good guy type that makes your skin crawl? Ezra is tall with dark hair, brooding eyes, a husky voice. There's always something going on behind his amber eyes, a world that I've wanted to be a part of since we met our freshman year of college eight years ago.

We had a general studies class together; at that time, Ezra had long hair and a squeaky-clean face. He was sitting at a table with his head down when I walked in; I was going to slip to a seat in the back of the class, but when his phone vibrated on the table next to him, he looked up and stole my heart. Not surprisingly, his Christian stuff has placed a wall between our hearts, romantically, of course, but at the very least, we're still good friends.

As I make it to the lobby, Ezra's black car pulls up to the front doors. I feel my heart double thump as I approach, but I ignore it yet again. At this point, I'm certain I have gas.

"Hey, Ez, thanks for coming," I say, sliding into his car.

He yawns and looks over at me. Those same amber eyes burn with an ethereal glow. They're always burning, but the college boy who stole my heart years ago somehow morphed into the man at the wheel before me now. Big hands cover the entire leather wheel, twin veins cross each other as they run up his strong forearms to hide beneath his pushed-up sleeves. Broad shoulders fill his seat, but what really makes me gush is the way his eyes always lock with mine. Dark brows and neatly trimmed facial hair adds to the mystery hidden in Ezra's eyes. Maybe it isn't mystery, just that he isn't as extroverted as I am.

"You say that like I had much of a choice."

"You did." I nod happily.

He rolls his eyes and pulls off. "I didn't. You would've held this against me, fought me so I wouldn't come see you off to Japan on Wednesday, and then you would've called me from Japan and told me how much I didn't like you, all because I didn't come do this." He waves a hand, and I laugh.

"What is *this*?" I pass a hand between the two of us. He glances down at me and then back out at the night traffic. I know the answer isn't the one I want, but I can't help myself. I want to be important to Ezra, important enough for him to abandon his faith for me. I want his love and attention, and he won't give me all of him because of his faith.

"This is a work in progress."

I snort to hide the bitter pain in my chest. "Not even a friendship?"

"Can we even call it that at this point? We've been friends forever, we're like," he pauses and shrugs.

Say it... say a couple.

"Family."

I clench my jaw, trying not to feel every negative emotion that storms through me. "Right. Family."

He glances over, but I look out the window.

"Hey, what's wrong?"

"Nothing, family member."

He laughs, and I wonder if he feels the connection and ignores it, or if he doesn't feel anything at all. Are we truly nothing more than two people who share a few interests and a few uninteresting memories?

"Goodness," he starts, "you want to be friends that badly? Fine, we're friends. Closeknit friends. Happy?"

"I thought you couldn't be friends with someone who's not Christian."

He huffs. "I told you, you're different."

"I'm the exception."

"You're the *assignment*," he corrects. Ezra always says that. He always says there's a purpose to our friendship, and one day, God will fulfill whatever purpose a friendship could have outside of ... friendship. I could start an argument that everything doesn't have to have a purpose, but Ezra will quote scriptures and tell me that everything in our lives serves a point. What we learn, what we make of situations, people we encounter. That's why his God is adamant about friends of the world being enemies to Him; friends with the world pull His children astray. Because everything that happens in our lives has some secret reason behind it... right.

I adjust in the seat, too exhausted to fight, and change the subject. "Where are you taking me to eat?"

"I was thinking Bailey's. They're open now."

"That diner with the chili fries?"

"Mmhmm." He nods.

"I like that place."

"I know."

I gaze at the side of his face. Perfect features on an eloquently carved plane. He holds a small smile as the night lights flicker across his face. When he slows to stop at a red light, he finally looks over at me. My breath hitches when our eyes meet. Ezra and I have so many moments like this. Silence, but our gaze doesn't break, the air is heavy, there are words to be said. But like now, the light turns green, and the moment passes. There's never enough time for us to say the things we want to say.

He clears his throat. "We're here."

"Finally." I click my belt free and hop out the car. Ezra comes around and I take his arm. He doesn't falter or hesitate. He doesn't make it known to me in any other way than our silent exchanges that there could be more to us than friends. He just lets me do what I want, but I want to know what *he* wants.

We step inside the quiet diner and seat ourselves. The red

and white tiles match every booth in the quaint place.

"What are you ordering?"

I raise a brow. "Fries, remember?"

"Just fries?"

"What else? I've got to stay in shape."

He laughs, and I chuckle to hide the butterflies he still gives me. "You're going to Japan; they eat much lighter than we do. You'll be fine."

"They eat some heavy stuff."

He shrugs. "Their heavy food is still not as heavy as American food."

"Can we please talk about something else?" I whine, tilting my head back to rest it on the backboard of the booth.

"What's wrong? I thought you were excited to go to Japan."

I shrug and sit up. "I was but now I'm not. I hate packing, and I hate flying. And I'll be there for two weeks." I press a palm to my head. "What was I thinking?"

"You were thinking of completing your dissertation."

"Sometimes I wonder why I'm even doing all this. Just trying to prove a point to a dead woman."

"Hey," he says roughly, but his betrayingly gentle touch is what gets my attention. I look down at his hand over mine. "There's not a child on this planet who hasn't wanted to prove their parents wrong. It's okay to struggle, you don't have to heal right away from losing your parents, but you do have to forgive. That's a choice. Healing is a process."

"I know," I say, "I know."

He lifts my hand across the table and kisses the top of it. Suddenly, I'm praying. Even though God and I aren't on speaking terms, I can't stop myself from hoping for more. Praying that just this once He would hear me and grant my request. *Please let things work out between Ezra and me.*

"Things are going to be okay; I promise. You'll get to Japan, and you'll love it," Ezra says, completely unaware of what's happening in my frazzled brain right now.

"And if I don't?"

"Then come home."

"You won't be disappointed that I didn't stay?"

He laughs. "No. I'd be disappointed that you didn't stay long enough to get me a souvenir, but I'll get over it." We laugh together, and I feel Ezra squeeze my hand once more. "It's going to be alright, Taye. I promise."

For some reason, Ezra's words make me uneasy. Like he knows something, or like I know deep within that this trip will change me, or us. The only question is if the change is for better or worse?

2

Dontaye

"This is it," I say as we stand at the entrance to the airport. In all of Colorado, neither Ezra nor I have anyone to say goodbye to. We have each other.

I'm alone because my parents are dead and I'm an only child. Ezra moved from New York to Colorado for college and ended up staying after landing a good job here. We have other friends—mine are from college, his are from college and work colleagues—but nothing compares to our friendship. We are each other's number one. Always. I'm certain Ezra pities me and my loneliness to some degree, but there's something in our friendship that keeps us close.

"Be careful out there," he says sternly. Ezra always gets stern whenever I leave for a trip. This isn't my first trip, and it won't be my last, but Ezra has been here for every single one. He's never gone with me, but he always sends me off and welcomes me home each time.

"I know," I say, then I repeat the warnings he always gives me like a father talking to his child. "Check my surroundings. Watch what I eat. Don't go off with strange people."

He rolls his eyes. "Dontaye, I'm serious."

"I know. I promise to call every night. Sheesh, you're not my parents."

"I don't have to be to make sure you're safe or that you make it back home."

"Don't I always?" I try to keep a brave face, but that overwhelming feeling of danger steadily grows inside me and Ezra's warnings suddenly add to the pile of fear sitting in my gut like a hot rock. I want to talk to him about this, share what I'm secretly feeling inside, but I know as soon as I open my mouth Ezra will start preaching about God's protector—or worse, he'll tell me not to go. As worried as I am, I don't want Ezra to try to convince me to stay. I'm not sure I could resist his pleading, so I swallow these troublesome nerves and offer a weak smile.

"You always come back," Ezra says. He lifts his watch and reads the time. "Alright, you'd better get going. Text me once you land and call me once you're in your hotel."

"I will."

Ezra helps me swing my heavy bag over my shoulder. "I'm going to miss you, Taye, so don't overstay."

I laugh. "I'll be home before you know it."

"You'll miss Thanksgiving, and Black Friday."

I shrug. "But I won't miss Christmas." I thrust open my

arms and reach for him. Ezra is much taller than me, so he leans down and pulls me into his embrace, almost off my feet.

"I'll be praying for you, Taye," he says into my fluffy afro hair.

"You always do." My voice is muffled against his shirt, but I know from the hum in his chest that he hears me. We remain like that for a moment longer, and I take advantage of the hug to breathe in his scent. He smells of the coming winter holidays—pine and chestnuts and, somehow, joy.

When I pull away, I blink away silly tears and stare over Ezra's shoulder. No birds, no clouds, just a tired blue sky. Not bright like the summer, it's hazy out, like winter is tired already. Ezra pats my shoulder and his warmth in this moment surrounds and nearly suffocates me, but I want that. I want this moment to last forever. I want Ezra's warmth to flush my nerves away, but the next second, Ezra takes a step back and waves.

"Have fun, Taye."

I bounce my shoulder playfully, pretending the place where his hand had been doesn't ache for his warmth again. "You know I will."

With that, I grab my suitcase and turn for the doors. Once I get there, I can't help but look back once more and wave. Ezra has one hand in his pocket, and he shifts his weight from one foot to the other before he lifts his hand and waves back. Saying goodbye breaks my heart, but this mission is important. I've got to do this. So, with one last look at my best friend, I turn and leave.

—❦—

The plane to Japan is tight. I waddle through the aisle with my bag close to my chest, hoping I don't bump anyone. I scan all the faces I pass, wondering which of them I'd see in Japan. Maybe none. That thought makes me suppress an eyeroll at all the meaningless things filling my head. I'm exhausting to deal with, even to myself.

When I find my seat, there's a woman sitting in the chair beside me, smooth brown skin like mine with fire engine red tipped hair. Her hair is pulled into a tight ponytail which immediately gives *me* a headache. With her head tipped down, I'm thankful she hasn't looked up and acknowledged me. I'm tired and I don't feel like talking, not after suffering through that goodbye with Ezra. Despite my exhaustion, however, I am curious about what has grasped her attention. As I sit, I steal a peek at the book in her lap, but I can't read any of the text on the pages, so I leave it at that and lean down to pull out my headphones. When that happens, the woman adjusts the book in her lap, flashing the title at me. **Jesus Saves.**

I could honestly fall over and die. Of course, on the most important mission of my anti-religious life, I'll be sitting next to the *one* religious person on the plane...

Okay, there's no telling who else is religious on this flight but what fortune for me to be placed next to someone reading a book about Jesus. I hold in the heavy sigh I want to release and sink into my seat. I practically shove my headphones over my ears and turn the music up so even if this woman ever lifts her head from her precious book, I'll be drowning in music.

I waste no time when I touch down. I rush to my hotel room in the hopes of dropping everything to go sight seeing, but jet lag hits me like a professional, and I fall prey to sleep deprivation. When I wake up, drowsy and disoriented, I do the one thing any normal person would do; I call Ezra.

"Hello?" Ezra's voice is groggy and heavy. It sounds nice.

"Ezra, you picked up?"

Of course he did.

"I was waiting for you to call, but you never did. I was starting to get worried."

I try not to smile as I toy with the fringes of the white blanket on my bed. "Well, no need for that." I downplay his worry to hide my excitement over it. "I'm here now, and I'm heading into the country today. There may not be much connection out there, so I'll be back in a few days, and I'll call you then."

He inhales deeply and I hold the phone a little tighter. I miss him…

"Alright, just be careful, Taye."

"I will."

"Ok, talk soon."

"I…" I gulp down the words I really want to say and tell him, "Yeah. Talk soon."

Hanging up the phone, I stare out the window at the

midday sun and wonder what I'm in for.

I walk into a quaint little shop. It's packed, but I'm still able to snag a seat in the back corner as more people file in. At first, I think everyone is here for the ginger tea and cute gingerbread men they serve seasonally, but I quickly learn everyone is here to marvel at the shop owner and two children I assume are hers. Everyone is staring at the kids carrying drink orders and plates of warm gingerbread to patrons. Their eyes follow the children like hawks, though they do not appear as predators. If anything, they look curious. And as I glance around the café, I see some of those curious eyes land on me, too.

The shop owner is a Black woman with natural red hair and strong muscular arms. She moves gracefully through the shop, giving commands to her crew and directing her children as they help serve tables. We have similar brown skin, but my hair isn't red, its dark as the polish on my fingernails and curls like the springs of a mattress. I am only momentarily stunned by the staring; I've travelled enough to know the world is not as diverse as social media would have us think. But it's places like this that offer a wonderful environment for tourists and natives to come together peacefully and enjoy each other's differences and similarities.

"Would you like to order?" The little boy asks as he comes over to my table. His skin is smooth like his mother's and creamy like his sister's. The tanned little boy who looks like a

14

cross between the people here in Japan and his mother, is very polite as he struggles with the pad of paper. His sister, who seems a little older, comes over and takes the pad from him. She gives him hers since there is less paper on it. When his moon shaped eyes reach mine, he blinks blankly at me, and I realize I haven't placed my order yet.

"Sorry, I'd like ginger tea with the gingerbread special."

He nods. "Coming right up."

This is the most diverse place I've been to since I arrived here in Japan. I'd always heard there was a lot of division in this country, and that was clear (even in the tourist areas) all of the bigotry melted the moment I stepped into these four walls.

All kinds of people are here from every walk of life. There are businessmen stuffing their faces before zipping out the door as quickly as they came in. There are school kids in uniforms, laughing with each other, passing smiles while they huddle together. In the opposite corner of the shop, there's a group of ladies sipping tea (no gingerbread), while the table beside them is mixed with people who are obviously tourists. They've got cameras on their laps, and bags piled around the table on the floor, tripping some folks standing in line, or making others stumble who are coming in to gawk at the Black woman with red hair.

I like this place a lot. It almost feels nomadic. There are maps hanging on the walls that lead to nowhere. Outlines of countries are marked on the tables but there are no destinations marked. Some of the maps are missing pieces along the walls, like there is a path to follow but no one could

15

confidently take it. Almost like you need to make your own path.

Not to mention the different vases of plants. There are some big vases of black bamboo growing tall like a fence around the front desk. The top of each table has a design that doesn't correlate with any of the other tables. Some are tourist spots in the world, others are just names of countries, there are some painted streets, like the table beside mine has **Route 66** painted on it. My table has a "dead end" sign painted on it. I almost laughed that I would get a meaningless table, but maybe it isn't so meaningless. I didn't get a destination or a street, I got a dead end.

Maybe it's a sign that I should give up, or that everything ends here. I sigh, *don't be an idiot, not everything means something.*

I look back out at the shop and take in the smiles and laughter. Everyone here is different in their own way, yet there's a feeling of camaraderie among the patrons. They sit at separate tables, but the laughter all blends together. They're kind to each other when someone rushes by or makes a mistake. It's warm here, and despite the warmth, this will only amount to a memory, nothing more, and maybe less once the memory is forgotten.

Would I one day forget all that I'm trying to prove? Would one day, the anger that I cleave to be a distant memory, or something I can't remember at all? I don't know what I want. How I feel right now is too important to forget, but what if something else comes along that's more important to remember... to *feel?*

16

A sigh slips from my mouth before I stand to my feet. I'm no longer interested in the gingerbread and warm tea, so I bump through the crowd as the only angry patron alive and leave that happy little place.

"Too much thinking," I say aloud once I'm out on the sidewalk.

"Not enough fun?"

I turn to find an old man on a cane. He's hunched over with crooked fingers that grip the slick wood in his hand.

"Excuse me?"

"Too much thinking, but not enough fun?" the old man repeats our brief conversation with a thick country accent. I was staying in Tokyo, but I wandered out to the countryside two days ago with a backpack and camping gear to see the difference between the two places. The countryside had been a little homier, but there was a lot of silence to the point of it being disturbing. Here in bustling Tokyo, there's nothing but moving people and entertainment. I hadn't planned to find much conversation considering what I came here for, but I wasn't about to come to Japan and not see one of its biggest cities.

That's why I'm surprised to see this country man here in the city. And an old one at that. "I should get going," I say as I turn back to the street, but the old man persists.

"I thought you were the one looking for conversation."

I look back at the old man who smiles up at me now. Unbothered by the bustling crowded streets of Tokyo, the old man focuses only on me. I'm not sure if I should feel worried or if I should walk away, but I don't feel nervous at all.

"What kind of conversation do you want with me, old man?"

He snorts. "The kind that might enlighten you."

"Enlighten me?" I chuckle. "Alright. What do you want?"

"Let's walk for a while, I'll tell you when we find some place quieter."

I take a step back, but he waves a hand with gnarled arthritic fingers. "If I were going to do something bad, I would've done it when you weren't aware of me. Not when you've stared at me long enough to notice my fingers and hunch. Pretty distinct markings which you could report if something were to happen to you." His smile widens. "I am no threat. I promise, my dear."

Without a fuss, I concede but I tell him as we step onto the crosswalk, "You shouldn't be proud of your hunch or your fingers."

"You shouldn't be proud at all when your spirit is dead."

I almost stop in my tracks, but I don't want to lose the old man in the crowd, and it isn't like there's going to be much room for me to stop. The crowds keep moving; everyone has somewhere to go, and they're not about to let me ruin that or stop them.

A dead spirit… The words seem to haunt me.

I choose not to say anything else as I walk behind the old hobbling man. He's patient as he maneuvers the crowd, nimbly squeezing through people and apologizing for taking up more space with his cane. Eventually, we walk until the city behind us gets quiet and the crowds thin out. The black top cripples and cracks until it's broken into the fine dust that creates roads leading to the countryside.

"Can we take a break?" I ask.

"Sure." The old man stops at a bus stop. It's painted an old green color that's been faded by the sun. The wood is chipped, and the glass windows are dirty and gritty. I don't care; I just need a moment to sit.

I flop onto the bench and the old man continues to stand. The world is quiet around us, and he disturbs it by pointing into the distance at a mountain. "That is where I'm taking you."

I raise a brow. "*Taking* me?"

"Leading you," he says politely. "You need to go there to wake up the dead inside of you."

"The dead inside of me." Part of me seems to wither at the implications. "Do you have any idea how insane you sound?" I snap at him, and then I try to calm down. "It was a mistake following you out here."

"You came because you want to know the truth." The old man turns from the mountain he'd been looking at in the distance. His wrinkled face stretches into a smile. "I saw you asking the people here about the gods of our ancestors and if those religious beliefs have negatively or positively impacted our small town."

I squint at him. I'd done some interviewing when I took a trip into the countryside. People out there are quiet and live simpler lives, unsurprisingly, most of them are also more closely connected to their heritage and still follow their religion.

"You were there?" I ask.

He nods. "I was. I listened and then I decided to make my way into the city in the hopes of finding you."

"You decided to make your way into the city? *Really?* Crowded Tokyo? And took a shot in the dark that you'd find me? You *followed* me!" I yell. But the old man only shakes his head.

"I didn't need to follow you. God told me where to find you and where to lead you."

My mouth goes dry. I want to combat him, but honestly, it's more believable that God led him than he followed me at his age. Besides, I wasn't here to prove that God doesn't exist, because He *does*. I'm here to prove that there is no need for Him any longer. He can stay in Heaven. Leave us alone. Stop placing all His rules and regulations on people who have finally figured out how to live happily and peacefully without Him. Even now, this old man is following His commands, but for what? It's fruitless. He's still old. Still got a hump in his back. Still got swollen arthritic fingers. What has God done for him?

"I don't want anything to do with Him," I say bitterly.

"He wants everything to do with you."

I roll my eyes. "Listen, I don't have time for this. I—"

"Please," the old man inches closer, "let me at least show you the shrine, if nothing else."

Lifting my watch, I sigh at the time and give the old man a nod. Seeing the shrine wouldn't hurt. As far as I know, shrines aren't Christian relics. "Fine, I'll see the shrine. I need pictures, anyways."

"Very well."

A rickety bus pulls up and when the old man and I get on, there's one seat filled with a woman. She's younger than the old man, but he sits beside her anyways. They resemble each other, possibly father and daughter, whatever the case, she definitely knows him because she gets off the bus with us and travels up the mountain with us, too.

At the foot of a passageway, the old man points to a sign written in Japanese characters. I feel like if I squint hard enough, I can almost understand what the characters are saying.

"Why does that sign look so funny?" I ask. I can't really describe what I feel or that looking at that sign makes me dizzy, but I know the old man likely has an answer.

"You'll be able to read it once you come down the mountain."

I frown. "What?"

He waves. "You'll understand later."

Without another word, I follow the old man and his presumed daughter up the mountain. The weather is chilly, but not cold enough for more than the sweater and jeans I'm wearing. The long grueling walk up the mountain is almost worth it just from the sights on the trail. But the real treat is the big red and black shrine within the walls of a cave. It's dimly lit, but there's a little altar inside where I assume sacrifices were left in the past.

"Come in," the old man says as his daughter helps me

cross over the cracked ground to the depths of the cave. "This is a rare shrine here in Japan. Hidden in the cave for those who are looking for it."

"Who'd be looking for a shrine in a *cave*?" I ask.

"Those who are seeking answers."

I roll my eyes and watch as the young woman grabs a plate from the altar.

"Take and eat," she says.

I stare at the silver plate. There's flatbread on it that looks like it is as ancient as the shrine itself. I really don't want the bread, but for the sake of the entire experience and coming all the way up this mountain, I eat it. I chew the sticky stale bread until I will it down.

The woman laughs and offers me a goblet—I've no idea where she got it from, but I don't really fight it because I'm dying of thirst trying to get this bread down. I can smell the wine before the deep flavor rushes over my tongue. It's sweet and strong. A crisp and refreshing flavor that makes my entire body shudder. Goosebumps pebble my skin, and my mouth goes numb. The cup in my hand feels weightless, and so does my phone in the other hand. I begin to sway on my feet, but I don't feel drunk. I don't feel dizzy either... I just feel tired... I feel... *really* tired.

3

Dontaye

I grunt, rolling over as a chill runs up my spine. I blink, but the darkness doesn't disperse. "Hello?" I call, slowly sitting up. My head throbs as I look around in the darkness. "Hello? Is anyone there?" I feel around the floor until my hand hits something cool. I snatch it up, hoping it's my phone, but it's a flashlight instead. I don't remember bringing a flashlight with me, but I click it on anyway because I'm not about to sit here in the dark.

As I shine the light around, I call again, "Did they leave me?" I look in every direction, but there's nothing here except solid rock walls. "Where's the shrine? Where... am I?"

Don't panic! I tell myself the moment my heart kicks up a beat. I take a stilling breath and shine the flashlight around. "I won't find anything if I just sit here... but I'm scared." My hands begin to tremble around the flashlight. My phone and bag are missing, and nothing I brought here is with me...

I blink at the spot on the wall where the light is shining. "What am I even doing up here?" My mind feels like it's slipping. "Must've hit my head." I reach up to touch my head. I'm expecting pain, but nothing comes. No pain could mean I didn't hit my head, and my mind *is* actually slipping. I shake my head. "No, just think, Taye. Why did you come up here?" I try to talk this out with myself, straining to remember. It feels like I'm trying to look into a closed off part of my mind, but I have no idea why it's closed off.

"Ok, chill out," I say to myself sternly... *sternly*... He always says...

For a second, I almost remember someone important to me, and it makes my chest tighten. I gasp for air and try to blink away my swelling tears. "Ok, I came up here for... for..."

I pause and look at the rock walls.

"A shrine!" I exclaim. Relief washes over me, and I say aloud, "Progress, Taye. Who brought you up here and why? Why would you be looking for a shrine?" My mind goes blank again and suddenly, my head starts to feel numb and fuzzy. "Wait... what did I just say? Where am I again?" I glance down at my flashlight. "When I first woke up, I was looking for something else. Not this..." I squeeze the flashlight in my trembling hands. Fear starts to work its way into my mind, seizing me right there. I sit still, hoping to focus, but I can't. I can almost see my memories fading by the second. Faces, thoughts, places, everything is slipping. It's like the harder I try to remember, the quicker the memories fade.

I fall forward and begin to cry on the cold cave floor.

"Where am I? What's wrong with me!?" I'm about to freak out when the sound of voices echo through the cave. "Hello!? Is someone there!?" I scream.

No one responds, but I can hear indistinct chatter somewhere further away. I rush to my feet and shine the flashlight around until I spot a path to follow. I jog the path through the cave until light peeks around the corner. Excitement runs a stream of heat through my frame at the sight of the light.

I'm not lost. *Someone could help me!*

I take the only turn in the cave and follow the light. I slow down as the mouth of the cave becomes clear. I drag my feet forward in awe, blinking out at the place before me. Even though I can't remember much, I know this isn't right.

This place isn't where I'm supposed to be... but where *am I supposed to be?* I feel the flashlight slip from my hand, but I don't try to catch it before it crashes to the ground.

A heavy-set woman jerks around at the sound and looks me over in one tick. "Great heavens! You'll catch your death out here dressed like that!" The woman squeals as she pulls off the fleece shawl she has wrapped over her shoulders.

"What?" I look down at my outfit, barely registering that I'm wearing jeans and a sweater. I'm not dressed for the winter, but I can't remember why not. "Where am I? This isn't... this isn't..." I pause. *Where was I supposed to be?*

"Honey, this is The Native," the woman says.

"The Native?" I shake my head. "No, I was supposed to be at a sh—" I stop. I can't remember the word. Something...

shh? Shine? *No...* I groan in frustration as I shove my hands into my hair and drop to my knees. There's a rush of cold and my eyes fall to the snow. White crystals shimmer in the fading sunlight as the sound of crunching snow comes closer.

"Rachel? What's going on?" a man's voice calls.

"I don't know, I just found this girl here. She's lost, I think."

I shoot to my feet, and snap, "I'm not lost! I just can't remember!"

"Alright." The man raises his leathery hands. "Easy ... easy. We're just trying to help, that's all." He places a hand on his chest, and says slowly, "My name's Charlie, this here's my wife, Rachel."

My eyes dart between the two. They both look like settlers. Charlie is wearing a big brown coat, but underneath I can see the red flannel and jean overalls. His scraggly blonde beard isn't long, but it is thick and full. And his wife Rachel is a heavy woman, but not wider than her husband. Her big pink jacket is dusted with snow, and she has a scarf tied around her dark hair. She extends a white gloved hand to me and says, "We just want to help, dearie. Do you remember your name?"

I nod. "My name's Dontaye Jackson."

"What a pretty name." She smiles. "Do you remember why you were in that cave or how long you've been there?"

"I ... I don't know. I woke up there."

"Woke up?" Charlie gasps. "Did someone leave you there or something? Did someone hurt you?"

"I don't think so. I can't remember."

26

"That cave is a dead end. Only this entrance, but there ain't no exit," Charlie explains. "You can only go in and out this way."

"I didn't. I know I didn't come in this way. I ... I woke up. And all I had was," I look down at the ground and pause, "that flashlight." But that flashlight is gone now... and the longer I stare at the snow, the faster the memory of it fades.

"A flashlight?" Charlie and Rachel look at each other. They look as mystified as I feel. The freezing air races up my spine and I draw into myself. "What's a flashlight?" Charlie asks.

"Am I going crazy?"

"Rachel, get that blanket around her, I'll give you my throw coat. We're close to home."

She nods as she steps forward, but I jerk away.

"No, don't touch me! HELP ME! Take me home!" I trip over a rock and fall into the cave. The freezing cave floor makes me jerk upright as my teeth begin to chatter. "What is happening to me... I can't remember anything." I look up at Rachel, the woman with a kind face. "Why can't I remember anything?" I can feel tears swelling again as the wintery world around me begins to blur.

Rachel gathers her big pink coat and kneels to wrap her fleece shawl around me. "I don't know, sweet pea, but I promise we'll figure it all out, alright?"

"I just want to go home. I feel like I'm supposed to tell someone something, I'm supposed to be doing something. But everything before waking up is a blur... I just know this isn't home."

"Well," Rachel adjusts and tightens the shawl around me, "can you let my home be your home until we find your real one? It'll just be temporary, but I can't leave you out in this cold."

The freezing air and falling snow are enough to convince me of her request, but her sweet demeanor and reassuring smile makes me feel like we can really figure everything out.

"Okay." I nod.

"Alright. Come on." She grabs my hands. "Up on your feet, now. All it takes is your first step to start going somewhere."

I blink… I've heard that before. *Those words were said to me when I was a child, but who said them? M-M-Mom—?*

"That's right," Charlie's voice snaps me from my thoughts, and I realize Rachel's been trying to help me stand. She pulls me to my feet as Charlie goes on, "My Rachel always tells me that."

"Charlie is always heading somewhere, but he gets a little fearful sometimes. Just got to remind him to start."

I force an obligatory smile of gratitude as Charlie helps Rachel into the carriage, and then me. The white horses trot off once Charlie pulls on the leather reins. I look around the blizzarding world of Charlie and Rachel in confusion. Despite how distraught I am, I can't help but take in everything around me. It feels like there's something strange in this world, something that's not only making me forget things and events but it's making me forget my problems, too.

The land is beautiful, like an old Christmas themed town. When I was a kid, my family would drive through Christmas towns during the holiday season, and we'd stare at the lights and eat candied apples and drink hot chocolate as we waited for Santa's train ride to come back around. This place is like that ... but on steroids.

There are bulls and oxen walking the snowy streets without reins or muzzles. White rabbits dart in and out of shops, bounding down the road while children dressed as eskimos skip around them. Mules and horses pull carts and carriages through the old town, ladies step out dressed in flowing gowns draped in parkas and furs with massive hats on their heads. Everything is wooden, from the house posts to the product displays in the small markets we pass. Log cabins, shacks, even stables. The air smells of peppermint and maple and it's electrified by a shocking sense of joy that threatens to shatter my confusion and fear.

I almost welcome it.

As strange as this place is, it is beautiful and I cannot get enough of it.

"Morning, Mr. and Mrs. Dais!" someone calls.

"Morning!" Charlie hollers to the woman standing in line at a tool shed and Rachel waves beside me. The small woman bundled up in a big puffy jacket with fur all over waves frantically. She even waves at *me*. I don't wave back, I just watch her as we pass by. I don't have it in me to be cheerful, to be happy. I don't know where I am and I don't know where I'm coming from, or where I've been.

I woke up in a cave. The worst possible place to wake up. And then I stepped out into the freezing world. This has to be a dream. There is no explanation for the memory loss and this old-fashioned winter wonderland. Maybe all I need to do is wake up. If I could just wake up, then I'd realize this is all a dream.

If I close my eyes, then maybe—

"Home sweet home!" Charlie's loud voice snaps me from my thoughts. My eyes open to a cabin; big wide logs hefted atop each other in different directions so it appears in a diagonal design. There's also a wraparound porch leading to a wide oak door with a golden handle.

"Come on." Rachel pats my hands in my lap. "We've got to get inside before the snow gets too—"

"When can I get help?" I ask without thinking.

Rachel presses her lips together. "It'll be a little while with the weather getting bad. But I promise once this storm passes, we'll take you up to the cabin in the mountains, and the Guardian there will be able to help you."

"The Guardian?"

She nods. "He's the one who enforces the Messianic Law around here and keeps us all safe."

My brows lower as I recite her words in my head. "Where have I heard that term before?" A pang zips through my head, and I cry out, dropping my head into my lap.

"Don't think too hard!" Rachel cries worriedly. "Come on, let's get inside." She grabs my arm and helps me out of the carriage and up the steps. With my less than limited options (because I had *no* options) I follow Rachel inside, trying not to make a fuss of the whole thing.

"Winter and Aconite! Come down here and give me a hand!"

"Coming!" two voices shout in sync.

"You can sit by the fireplace, pinecone, and I'll bring you some jellied toast and cocoa."

It takes me a minute to realize she's talking to me—I've never been called a pinecone before—but when Rachel pats my shoulder, I take the hint and wobble to the fireplace.

In the living room, I stand there blinking at the crackling flames. The stone wall surrounding the fire looks shabby, but the warmth makes up for the aged place. The flames are vibrant and strong, and they dance with each other in the confines of the fireplace. The house smells of sugar and chocolate and my stomach growls at the thought of Rachel's cocoa and toast. If I open my mouth, I'm sure I could taste it.

There are candles dotting the walls, wafting a fragrance of cranberries and wine into the air, and the floor is covered by cozy furs. On the walls are antlers, wreaths, and there are honest-to-God chestnuts roasting over the open fire. I don't know what to make of this place. Everything here looks familiar, like I've seen this before, or if I could just remember, it almost feels like I've *lived* here before. That empty feeling of not remembering who you are besides your name or where you came from is exhausting.

As exhausting as my dissertation. I chuckle to myself and then squeal, "Wait!" as if I'm speaking to the person taking my memories away. As if yelling will make the memories stop fading.

I drop to my knees and tears immediately fill my eyes as my mind goes blank again. Slapping a hand over my mouth, I try to hold in my sob as Rachel stumbles around the corner in a white apron.

"What's wrong?" she coos, kneeling beside me.

"I ... I remembered something... but it's gone again!" I throw myself onto her, and she holds me.

Gently rubbing circles in my back, she says, "Sometimes it's hard to remember. It comes in fleeting moments. But don't let that break you. One day, those moments will stay a little longer, until eventually, you're all pieced together."

"But when!?" I cry as I jerk from our embrace. "When will it all come together!? I can't stay here forever! I need to go home *now*!"

"I'm so sorry, marshmallow. All I have is my word right now. And I know you don't know me," she reaches out and wipes my many tears, "so my word may not hold much weight. But I promise you, God's going to work this out. Just you wait. Give Him a little time, alright?"

God... I remember Him... clearly. All I remember is not believing anyone should follow Him... but why not?

"I'm not... I'm not religious," I whisper. "I remember that. I don't believe in God."

"That's alright, He believes in you. And it might not be so bad to believe in Him right now, right?" She shrugs, maintaining her gentle smile. "When you've got nothing else, when you're at your lowest point, why not turn to Him?"

She's right… but I can't remember why I'm not religious. I just know that I'm not and that is stopping me from wanting to try to believe, though her words are stirring me.

"Just think about it, alright?"

I nod. "Okay."

"Alright now, my twins are gonna come in here with your food while I run out back and make sure the stables are ready for this storm with Charlie. Just holler out that window, there." She points right across the room to a little window carved into the logs. "I'll come running."

I smile. "Thank you, Rachel."

She pulls me into a hug and pats my back. "It'll be just fine, cinnamon."

As she stands to her feet, she unties her apron and calls, "Winny, Nite, get this girl her toast and don't ask any questions. I'm going out to help your father reinforce the stables, got it?"

"Yes ma'am," the two little voices call together.

I huff as I wipe my tears and turn back to the fireplace. Maybe Rachel's right, I should pray, but I just don't want to. I don't want to do anything but go home.

I pull my knees to my chest to rest my chin on them when the padding of little feet echo through the room.

"Hi there," a small voice calls.

I look over to find two children dressed alike standing six feet away. One's holding a tray, the other's holding a metal mug. The two children are twins, identical. They look neither male nor female with how similar they are in appearance. Sporting big blue eyes like Charlie, and dark hair like Rachel, the only way you can tell them apart is the pair of earrings one of them is wearing. Little pendants shaped like Christmas trees.

"Hi," I say softly.

"Mommy says you have to eat." The twin with the mug steps forward and offers it to me.

"Thank you." I say, taking the mug.

"This is my brother. I'm the sister," she pats her chest, and I nod mutely.

The little girl glances back at the other twin and stamps her foot when he doesn't move. He's been standing there gawking at me, but at the stomp of his sister's little foot, he jerks forward and brings me the toast. I offer him a smile, and he immediately lets go of the tray and hides behind his sister.

"Nite is very shy," she says, "but I'm not."

"That's good."

"So," she grabs her brother's hand and pulls him over with her as she sits beside me. "Are you moving in?"

"I don't know yet."

"Mom's going to make you do chores if you do." She laughs.

"Oh."

"Don't worry, Momma's really nice. And so is Pa."

"Your parents are lovely."

"What about your parents?"

"Mom said not to ask any questions," Nite says with panic in his voice.

34

I try to force a smile. "It's okay."

Winter looks worried now, glancing from her brother to me.

"I don't," I pause to swallow the lump forming in the back of my throat, "I don't remember my parents. But I'm sure they were lovely."

"Probably. All parents are good, at least I think so," Winter says as she smiles at me.

I give her a nod. "You're probably right."

Her smile grows bigger, and the sight of the twins lets me escape my own problems for a little while. The two of them get comfy on the floor beside me, sitting by the fire, asking me questions, and not shying away even when I don't have answers.

At least for now, this is okay.

4

Dontaye

It's been five days, and I've slept every night. Which means I haven't been dreaming. Unless you can sleep in dreams. *Can you sleep in dreams?* Can you wake up and keep living the same life in dreams? If you accept a dream as reality, will you ever wake up?

I sigh as I adjust on the bed. The dark thoughts always seem darker and stronger at night. At least the bed is soft, despite the layer of straw beneath the wool. Rachel gave me Nite's bed and makes him sleep on the couch for the time being. He doesn't mind at all since he loves the fireplace. Winny and I are sharing the room she normally shares with her twin brother. It's small, but it's better than nothing.

The cold night whispers a chill through the room, and I sit up to check on Winter. The little girl is sleeping, clutching a raggedy stuffed bear. I can't tell if the chill reached her, but it certainly reached me, and I can't stay in bed any longer because of it.

As I climb from the bed, I check the firepit in the middle of the room. There's a small flame eating away at some wood chips covered in soot. Pulling on one of Rachel's house coats she lent me, I head out for wood. Winter, the older twin, told me that Charlie and her grandfather built this house long before she was born. Her parents intended to have only one child but ended up with two—which explains why the bedroom is a little tight for two people. She also told me where to find the firewood. She and Nite always go together to collect the wood when their bedroom gets too cold. Sometimes they don't need to if Charlie leaves extra wood outside the bedroom or comes in through the night to change the wood. He doesn't do it as much now since they've gotten a little older.

I try to stay quiet as I creep through the house. Since I've been here, the snow hasn't let up at all and there's been no word on how much longer the snowstorm will last. No one can travel in these conditions to relay any messages. This isn't just bad for me; I overheard Rachel and Charlie discussing pulling out some frozen meat they have stored away to get us through another few days. Rachel isn't concerned about food the way Charlie is. She's concerned about the other essentials getting low, like wood and oil and animal feed. Charlie's struggled out to the stables once to check on the horses, but it was so bad that Rachel had to go out and find him to bring him back home.

It's been hard for everyone for different reasons. I try not to let my own complaints weigh me down and drag down the family, but it's hard when nothing about this place makes sense yet it makes so much sense at the same time. It feels like I'm lost in a world that I've been in before. I just don't recognize it.

Moving through the dark house, I spot the cellar doors already open. Taking one of the burning candles from a holder on the wall, I hold it over the cellar entrance. "Is someone down there?" I whisper.

I hear Nite before I see him. He's dragging a green bag full of wood behind him as he reaches the bottom of the stairs. "I was getting wood," he says shyly.

I head down the stairs. "I'll help you carry the bag."

He shakes his head and grits his teeth as he pulls the sack further onto his shoulder. "I can carry this. I'm strong." Puffing his chest, he marches up the steps, though it takes him a while. I stay close to him, so he won't fall. Winter told me that Aconite said I was the prettiest woman he's ever seen. She squealed when she said her brother wanted to marry me. The two of them are the only reason I haven't lost my mind in all of this.

It's dizzying trying to remember day in and day out where I came from or something from my past. I haven't given up, it's only been five days, but five days of mental gymnastics is tiring. I'm not eating, just doing my best to sip water when I feel dry. I'm barely sleeping, just lying awake blinking at the ceiling, trying to stay quiet so I don't wake Winter. And I don't do anything. I sit by the fireplace and tend it when needed. The only thing I want to do is go home, wherever home is. Nite asked me once how I knew my home wasn't here, I couldn't give him an answer. Because there was this feeling that I belong here, or I need to be here. No matter how much I want to go home. Yet, I know this isn't home.

When we make it to the top of the stairs, Nite sets his sack down with a huff.

"Nice job, Nite," I say as I pull the cellar doors closed. I tie the rope around the handles as Charlie instructed. He said sometimes a heavy wind could push the doors open, and three years ago, Winter fell into the cellar when she was playing with her brother. She broke her arm but was fine otherwise. Since then, he's kept the cellar closed if no one's down there.

Nite pulls out two pieces of wood for me. I thank him and he drags the bag to the main fireplace to fill it again.

"Taye! Taye! Wake up!" Winter yells from her bed.

"What is it?" I ask sleepily. For the first time since I've been here, I was sleeping peacefully, and Winter woke me right up.

"The snow stopped! Mom says you can go see the Guardian now!"

I sit up out the bed and look around. There are no windows in our room, so I snatch my housecoat and race out the bedroom door with Winter on my heels. She grabs my hand and pulls me around to the window near the fireplace. "Look!"

she exclaims. Charlie is out back cleaning off the stables, and when I glance outside, I can see sure enough the snow has finally stopped. Two days had passed since Nite and I went to the cellar for firewood. I've been here an entire week, and now, I'm finally getting out of here.

"Where's your mom?" I ask Winter.

"She's making breakfast, come on!" She grabs my hand again and I can hardly contain myself as we run to the kitchen with Winter's voice calling for her mother. Rachel rounds the corner just as we are and Winny and I slam on brakes, trying to avoid a collision with Rachel.

"Mrs. Dais," I say with short breaths, "can we please go to the Guardian?"

Rachel chuckles. "Let me finish breakfast, and I'll take you right there, as promised."

I gasp and throw my arms around her which makes her giggle. Rachel has been good to me, treating me like one of her own children. This entire family has been good to me, and it's a bittersweet feeling to leave them all, but going home and returning to my normal life with my normal memories is all I want.

The twins give me big hugs, but Rachel tells them I'll only be able to gather information today. I can't leave quite yet, but an investigation into how I got here and how I'll get home will begin, and that was good enough for me. Knowing I can go home, and I'm not stuck here will bring me unfathomable relief.

Charlie gives me a hug, too, and he tells me when I come

back, he'll show me the stables, and if I'm up to it, he'll let me help out with the horses, so I'll have something to do. I don't have any experience with horses, at least I don't think so. But I don't tell him that, instead I just nod.

"Now," Rachel says as we hitch a ride on a mule's cart. Since Charlie's horses don't like the mountains and that's where the Guardian lives, a friend of his lent us his mule and cart for our travels. "The Guardian can be a little hard to deal with sometimes. He's a very busy person, handling an entire town's needs. It's hard since he's been the only one chosen for this position in a while."

"The Guardians are chosen?" Rachel nods, so I add another question, "Why are they called *Guardians*?"

"Because they look after this place," she says. "They take care of all of us and make sure this place stays safe."

"I see." My eyes drift to the beauty of the mountainside. The translucent snow reflects the light in a shimmering rainbow. Evergreen trees are heavy with thick white snow that looks like clouds resting on the branches. The mountaintop has the same heavy white fluff rolling down to the crevices of its frame.

The beauty of this world is unmatched. It feels like everything here is purposely beautiful to gather my attention. It feels like I'm the only one who sees the beauty here, or maybe everyone else is used to it. For some reason, I can't shake that this world is calling to me in every way possible. From the familiar house to Rachel and her family, even the snow and this mountain, it all feels like there's some part of me mixed into all of it. I can't explain why a mountain might be part of me, it's just what I feel. Which could be totally backwards since I can't remember anything except my name and that I'm not religious.

When we arrive at the small log cabin, I can feel the hope I had on the way up the mountain melting through my feet. I was expecting the place to be a little more attractive to the eyes, just like the rest of this world. But the cabin looks shabbier than anything I've seen thus far. It looks out of place, nothing like where a Guardian of an entire city would live or work.

"Uh, why is this place not the best in town?"

"Makes you wonder if anything good can come from here, doesn't it?" Rachel smiles coyly, and I feel like I should understand what she's referencing but I don't. Her words sound familiar, but everything here sounds and looks familiar, so I can't place it.

The bell dings as we step into the warm cabin. A small woman with skin brown like cocoa glances up from the big front desk she is sitting at. "Hi," she greets us flatly. "If there's a blockage, you'll have to wait a little while. We do ask that all townsfolk try to carve their way out before coming to the Guardian."

"Oh no," Rachel fans a thick hand that's free from the pink gloves she's been wearing. "We're just fine. But we do need to see the Guardian. This young woman is lost, and she can't find her way home. Woke up in a cave," Rachel adds hesitantly.

The woman looks from me to Rachel like she doesn't

believe us, but doesn't really care enough either, so she complies and says, "I'll let him know someone needs to see him."

Rachel thanks the woman before she leaves to go into an office right behind her desk. I don't get to peek inside when she goes in or comes out, but there are enough oddities around the dank cabin to keep me occupied. Like all the carvings on the walls. They tell the story of a small girl and a winged creature. The winged creature watches over her until she grows up and looks beyond him. He turns her heart to the clouds, and she reaches for them. But oddly enough, that's where the story ends.

How weird, I think to myself as the door to the office opens. I clutch Rachel's hand excitedly and sit straight up. I can feel the rush of anxiety flowing over me as I realize I am that much closer to getting home.

A young man makes his way around the desk, stopping to greet the lady there, before returning his attention to us. Without thinking, I slowly stand, not caring that Rachel's hand slips from my grasp.

The young-looking man is wearing a navy-blue cropped sweater that is full and heavy and branded with a golden patch that has the word *Guardian* stitched on it in white. His midnight pants are neatly tucked into the shiniest black boots I've ever seen. Hanging off his shoulders is a thick cape that dusts the floor, the length of his tall strong frame. And he has a familiar face. One I can't stop staring at. My brain is trying to work as fast as my heart pumps to find the memory of him. My eyes recognize him, but my brain can't recall where from. My heart feels everything he's always made me feel, but as usual, my mouth can't find the words to say.

His thick dark hair and bright eyes that stir with something majestic behind them are making me dizzy right where I stand. He looks perfect, as if the earth called for a guardian angel, and not a man. Perfect in every way, from his glistening skin to his chiseled jaw, and wide shoulders. The only thing he's missing is a pair of wings.

The Guardian stops close enough to intoxicate me with his ethereal beauty and earthy scent, like pine and mint and joy. The hammering in my chest won't give me a break. *He's important to me*, I think to myself. Now that I'm standing, something tries to resurface. The knowledge that there is a chasm between this man and myself, but I am desperate enough to cross it... I just can't remember why I never did.

I take one shaky step closer and out of nowhere, I whisper, "Ezra?" It's the name of the man who was perfect for me. His name is strong enough to summon his silhouette in my mind, bringing the image of someone I thought I knew before my eyes. But when I blink, the image is gone, and so are all the stirring feelings. I can hardly remember what I just felt. But it was strong.

"Taye? You alright?" Rachel asks as she stands. "Sorry, she's been dizzy ever since she woke up."

The Guardian's eyes flee from mine for just a second to acknowledge Rachel. When his eyes return, he offers me his hand. "Yonah Adelle, Guardian of The Native."

I hesitate before I place my hand in his. "Dontaye Jackson."

"A wonderful name for the new Belle of The Native."

Time stands still for just one second when our hands touch. There's a feeling that stirs at the contact, like I'm living out a fantasy of the boy I can't remember, in a perfect world we can't escape.

"Ahem," Rachel clears her throat and Yonah and I drop our hands. "We're here for help, Yonah," she says flatly.

"Sorry, Mrs. Dais, I was only introducing myself."

Rachel's only answer is a raised brow.

"Well," Yonah continues, "why don't you two come into my office and we'll talk."

"I needed to run some errands, actually, but now I don't know if I can leave you two alone."

"Come now," Yonah laughs, "I'm a Guardian, Rachel. Ms. Jackson's safety and wellbeing is my utmost concern."

"Mmhmm," Rachel sasses. She grabs my hand which takes my attention from the handsome Guardian. "Despite his antics, you're in good hands. I'll be back to get you soon, alright?"

I nod. "Thank you, Rachel."

She smiles as she pulls me into a hug. "And remember, no matter what, Nite is willing to sleep on that couch no matter the length of time."

I chuckle. "You've been very kind. All of you, I hope this isn't it, but…" I bunch my shoulders, and she laughs knowingly.

"Oh, there's no place like home. Go for it." Hugging me once more, Rachel gives Yonah that fierce raised brow before taking her leave.

"She's sweet, isn't she?" the young Guardian asks beside me.

"Most certainly."

"Come, let's chat first, then I'd like to show you all of The Native. Well, all of what I can show you before it gets too late. The Native is quite a land to see."

"I'm sorry, I didn't come here for you to take me on a tour, I came for help." I glance at the secretary who looks back down at her work immediately. "I want to go home."

Yonah steps forward, his leather boats thumping against the shining oak floors. He looks even more angelic up close. "Ms. Jackson, I'm afraid I won't be able to get you home at this time." He pauses. "You're not ready to go home."

"Wait, so this *isn't* my home! I'm *not* crazy!?"

"Nope." He shakes his head, a smile capturing his lips. "Not at all. The Native is not your real home. Come, I want to show you something." He turns and leads me out of the cabin, but I just stand there. I can't get my legs to move. Even as the cold air whisks in and roves over me, the Guardian's words are only just now processing, and it isn't making sense.

Yonah is still holding the door open when he glances back and notices I haven't moved. "Ms. Jackson, what I want to show you is out here."

"I don't," I swallow, "I don't understand."

"But you will." He turns and comes back inside. When he

grabs my hands, I can feel his warmth even through our gloves. Bright eyes search my own for a moment before he says, "Please, Ms. Jackson, let me show you this world, and you'll begin to understand." He gently tugs on my hands, and absently, I move. I'm not really thinking anymore, just moving because he's pulling me along.

When he opens the door again, the freezing air zips by, sending a chill up my spine. I follow in a stupor behind him, but the Guardian doesn't let my hand go. I feel dizzy thinking that for some reason I'm not home, but I can't go home either.

We walk to the edge of the mountain in silence.

"Look over the edge and tell me what you see."

"I don't want to look," I refuse. "I want to go home. If none of this is my home, then I don't care to see it. I want to see my home." I rip my hand from his and shove it into my chest. "MY HOME! I want to see my bedroom! My home! My place! The people I love! I don't want this!" My words come out in a scream torn from within. A hook jagged and cutting through my body to spring free as a cry of pain. A cry of defeat, and hopelessness. The despair that tumbles over me sends shards of heat and coolness through my body. I'm desperate for a place I can't remember. But that doesn't matter. It's my home and I want to be *there*. Not here.

I drop to my knees in the snow, digging my fist into the thick white blanket that chills me to my bones. Why does it hurt so badly? To be stuck in a place where I can't remember anything should've been easy to adjust to. But the only things I've forgotten are the memories, not the way the memories or the people from them made me feel. There's someone I love, someone I hate, grief I never addressed, anxiety I'd fought every day. But I can't pinpoint anything more than feelings, though I try and desperately want to.

"WHY?" I scream as I pound my fist into the snow. "Why can't I just go home!"

"Because there is so much you must learn before you can go home."

"*Learn?*" I snap my head up to see Yonah looking out at the edge of the mountain. "What am I supposed to *learn?* You can't keep me here! Someone will come looking for me!" I nod to myself before violently wiping my nose. "Someone will come looking for me."

"I doubt that," he says sarcastically.

"I *don't.* I know I have people who care about me that will look for me."

"I don't doubt that." He turns to face me. The thick velvet cape hanging from his broad shoulders moves with his motion, as if the cape is dusting the snow from his boots. "The only thing I doubt is that they'll come looking for you." He extends a hand to me. "Ms. Jackson, time doesn't work the same way here as it does where you're from."

I stare at his hand. "What?"

He chuckles and hikes his pants up to squat in front of me. His cheeks are peach pink, and his nose is strawberry as he explains, "The Native is a spiritual world created just for you."

My tears slow down as confusion and clarity fight within me.

"You were brought here by God," the Guardian says.

"By God? That's impossible. Of everything I've forgotten, I still remember that I'm not religious."

"Isn't that funny?" He smiles brightly. "The only thing you remember, and are certain of, is that you weren't religious. Who else would bring you to The Native?" He pauses. "You can't answer because you don't remember your world. That's what's tricky about this place, but it's all God's doing."

"Why would God, who I have no association with, bring me here? *Trap* me here! Do you think I'm crazy enough to believe that?"

"Not crazy, but what else will you believe? There's no way in or out of The Native. That's why I brought you here, at the highest peak in the land, where you can see everything, even the barriers on each side."

I stare. "What are you talking about?"

"Come." He takes my hand. "I'll show you."

Once he helps me to my feet, we walk to the very edge of the mountain, and he points ahead. I follow his hand as he thrusts it across the expanse. There are barriers just as he said, crystal walls that are nearly transparent if it wasn't for the sparkling light emitting from them. One small village is set between four mountains, that is all of The Native.

"How?" I whisper. "This doesn't make sense. How can I be trapped in a spiritual world?"

"You're not trapped, you're asleep."

My brows lower as I turn to him. "What did you say?"

"You're asleep, on the other side. The Native is your

dream world where you've been sent to learn about God."

"I'm *asleep?* So, you're telling me that my real body is out there somewhere?"

"I'm telling you that the cave you woke up in was a replica of the one you've fallen asleep in within your world. The entire Native is a replica of your world."

I push him away as I back up. "No, this is crazy. I refuse to believe this." I snort as I try to take a breath. "If I'm asleep, then I can jump off that edge and die and wake up."

"Not exactly." Yonah turns to look out again and says over his shoulder, "The dream realm is God's opportunity to communicate with people when they are closed off to Him. Or when they're too busy for Him. Sometimes He communicates through dreams because God is a God of symbolism, just like Jesus told stories in parables." He turns back to me. "This dream is meant to draw you closer to God when you awaken, just like the parables were meant to draw the nonbeliever to seek out Christ."

The dizziness starts again, and I take a wobbly step back from the edge I'd just threatened to throw myself over. "I don't feel well. I can't breathe. I'm hot." I rasp as I rip off my gloves. I tear my hat from my head and try to unzip my jacket.

"Stop," the Guardian says, but when I don't listen, he blurts, "It's freezing! You're going into shock!" The Guardian's voice calls to me, but I can't focus as a world of darkness washes over me.

5

Dontaye

My head throbs the moment I open my eyes. My entire body feels weak as I try to turn over in bed.

"Don't move too much," Rachel's voice comes gently. "I just changed your rag."

I reach up and feel the warm rag on my head. "What happened?"

"You ran yourself a fever after hearing some news from Yonah."

I squint. "The Guardian?"

Rachel nods as she moves from her spot in her rocking chair to sit on my bed. "He's here, you know. Just stopped by to check on you. Do you want to see him?"

I bunch the blankets in my hands as I look down at the bed. Unfortunately, passing out and running a fever hasn't eliminated the memories of what the Guardian told me.

In a whisper, I say, "Yes."

"You sure, sweet pea? Because I'll tell him you need more rest."

"I need to understand what's happening."

Rachel pats my hand with a nod and leaves the room. I pull the rag off while I lay there waiting, trying to go over all that Yonah told me. He said this world, The Native, was a dream world. Which is actually a spiritual world God created for me. According to Yonah, God uses the dream world to communicate with people all the time. Which is why everything has felt so purposeful and why everything feels like it's part of me. Because it is ... in some way.

I don't know what each part of this world represents, but everything around me links back to the real world. God did that so I can connect the dots when I wake up and see Him in every area of my life.

The only reason I believe any of this is because I'm *not* religious. Yonah pointed out that the only thing I remember about myself from the real world, besides my name, is that I'm not religious. Why remember *that*, out of my entire life's experience? Something I never thought was important. Or maybe being nonreligious in my real life *was* important. Either way, it unfortunately makes sense that this would be God's doing.

"God," I say quietly, "why me? Why a nonreligious person? Why come after someone who doesn't want to be found?"

The door opens, cutting my conversation short. I don't

know if He's going to answer, but it's worth a shot to ask the Source after all.

Yonah walks inside the room wearing his sweater and cape, his heavy boots and leather gloves.

"Are you always on duty?" I ask.

He chuckles. "Technically speaking, yes. I am the sole Guardian of The Native, I am always watching over."

"Is that why you came here?"

"To check on a fellow Native." He smiles. "How are you?"

I shrug, suddenly annoyed by the Guardian's cheerfulness. "Look around, Guardian, what do you think?"

Yonah follows my sarcasm and glances around. When he finds nothing, he looks back at me with a weak smile. I almost roll my eyes. Yonah moves through the small room; he takes up so much space, the room feels tighter with him in it. He stands over Winter's bed and lays his gloves on it before unclasping his cloak and turning to lay it over me. The scent that rolls off his cloak fills me with delight. Something sweet under the husky and manly scent makes me shiver in warmth.

"This is heavy," I choose to complain, despite his warmth. How I feel for the Guardian is eerily similar to something I know I've felt in the real world. That tension in my chest, and sudden annoyance because I'm too childish to tell him how I feel. I've experienced this before, and I hate that I am experiencing it again with him.

"Heavy are the shoulders that bear the news of Truth."

I stop squirming beneath the massive cloak as Yonah pulls

the rocking chair beside my bed. "I'm sorry all this has been so hard on you. It's been hard on me, too, seeing you like this."

I shift in the bed to try and sit up.

"Let me help you," he offers.

"No, I want to do it myself."

"You don't have to do everything alone, Dontaye," he says as he ignores my request and leans over me. He is even more regal up close. Long fluffy lashes, and an aura of light beam around him as he slips his hands beneath me. "Grab onto my shoulders," he says softly. He really doesn't have to tell me twice. I can pretend for years that I hate Yonah, but not now when he's this close with this kind of contact.

I wrap my arms around his large shoulders and hang on as he lifts me in the bed with ease. He sits me against the headboard and asks, "Is this alright?"

"Yes."

When he pulls away, a lonely chill crawls over me as my heart races like a wild horse. Yonah sighs and sits in the rocking chair. His long legs and tall frame fill out the entire chair in a different way from when Rachel sits in it.

"You know, there's more to The Native that might help you understand all of this."

"Will it bring my memories back?"

"No, but it's not supposed to. Your memories are repressed for a reason and with great cause."

"Why would a *loving* God do this to me?"

Yonah sits forward, resting his elbows on his knees. "*Because* He's loving."

"You cannot be serious. Yonah, I'm trapped."

"You're sleeping."

I raise my hands and take a breath. None of this is Yonah's fault, but it is annoying that he sees no crime in this. "I know that I'm asleep, but…" I sigh. "Never mind, you wouldn't understand."

Yonah sits back and begins to rock in the chair. It squeaks against the wooden floor, and his leather boots make a muffled and tired noise as he rocks himself. I can't get myself to look at him, I don't want to. I don't want him to smile and say this is all a learning experience. I want him to tell me how to get home, but I know he won't.

In the silence, I grow comfortable and let my hands move over the thick fur of the Guardian's velvety cloak.

"Everyone in this world you've met before or will meet in the future, except this family," Yonah began to explain.

I long for him to stay quiet, but instead of snapping, I just let him talk.

"The Dais family serves a purpose to the secret pain you have locked away. Everyone else is a person in your life from your past or even your future."

"Ok." I fold my arms over my chest. "Let's say that I believe you, then tell me why this is happening to me?"

"God wants to reach you."

I huff. "I know, but why? Or why like this?"

Yonah leans back in the chair and closes his eyes. "God designed the world so that the invisible directly impacts the visible. The unseen God is the author of the world we can see, feel, touch, and experience." He holds up a finger as he slowly opens his eyes. "Yet, we have to bundle up because the invisible wind brings a chill. We have to let our bodies fight the things we cannot see internally. And we, who are very visible beings, have to breathe very invisible air or we'll die. That's amazing, isn't it?" He's looking at me now, wanting me to agree, but I don't. I don't care about any of that. I just want to understand *why me*.

"I can't do this," I say. I sink against the headboard and squeeze my eyes shut, hoping that when I open them, I'll be back in the real world… that does not happen, of course.

When I open my eyes, Yonah gives me a smirk and says, "I'll tell you a secret."

I grunt. "What?"

"There are two reasons you can't remember anyone or recognize anyone; the first is because God has blocked your memory."

"Obviously." I toss a hand up.

"Let me finish," he says. "God chose you because everyone deserves a chance to experience His love firsthand. So, He brought you here and gave you a blank slate to start with, without all the outside distractions or your real life's memories. Here in The Native, you have a chance to come to Him so when you wake up, and all the memories return, you'll know God's love, and you can make an informed choice to love Him back or deny Him." He opens a hand and flexes his fingers. "It's like a trial run. You spend time here, getting to know God without your memories or your past, and then you do the real thing when you wake up."

"But why take away my past just to give it back? My problems aren't getting solved, He just wants me to get to know Him. So why take the past?"

"Because people rely on past experiences to understand and provide solutions to future problems or problems in the present. If your life's experiences have been only what *you've* done without encountering God to know how He does things, then you'll never truly know God or what He'd want you to do." I try to remain neutral, but my ears are yearning for more. The more Yonah explains, the more I understand. "God wants you to experience Him and this was the only way He could grab your attention without your interference."

"The only way God *Almighty* could get my attention is by sticking me here?" I raise a brow like I finally beat the Guardian for once, but he replies, "Just shows how stubborn you are, and how relentless God's love is, doesn't it?"

There I was thinking my words would catch Yonah off guard, but they don't. His answer only proves that there is no way to get an upper hand over a servant of God.

"One day, all of this will disappear. It'll become a lost memory because you'll have created new ones of you depending on Christ in your world. This will be a dream you can't remember." He pauses. "It won't happen right away, but it'll be soon after you wake up. What you'll always hold with you, is that you experienced God's love. You'll remember Him, not us."

My eyes leap from Yonah's cloak to his strong frame

relaxing in the chair. "I don't want to be here, but I don't want to forget you guys, either."

"Well," he pulls his shoulders together, "I don't make the rules, beautiful. He does. And it won't matter. Like I said, everyone here is someone you've met or will meet in the future."

"The Dais are teachers, and everyone is someone I'll know or already know, does that also include you?"

He smiles. "Of course, that's why I'm the Guardian of The Native." He sits forward and locks eyes with me. "Or your native."

"*My* native? What's that?"

"Do you know what *native* means?"

I shrug. "No."

"Well, I'll tell you a little later when you're ready to hear about it."

"Just tell me now."

"Can't," he says playfully, offering me his charming smile again, "but I can tell you the second reason why you can't remember anyone or anything."

"I guess that's better than nothing."

Standing to his feet, he moves for Winter's bed to retrieve his gloves as he explains, "You can't remember anything because places and things are connected to people. Even most of our experiences are connected to people. The fun times and the good times. So, if you can't remember people, you can't remember a lot of other things, either."

"Ok, but that only tells me what I already know."

"Very good," he says without looking up from his gloves as he tightens the gold buckle around his wrist. "We take people for granted, especially the ones closest to us. The people we see every day, we can never imagine our life without them, yet we don't always cherish the moments we have *with* them. But the people we see less often, it's easier to remember them when they impact us. They're normally people we'll never forget."

I sit still, reflecting on Yonah's words as he clasps his other glove. "I think I understand," I say softly. "I can't remember anyone because their faces are so familiar. They are people I see possibly every day, but haven't quite relished them, not as I should have."

"Exactly. The ones closest to you are the ones that are the hardest to remember yet the ones you'll want to remember the most." Yonah comes around the bed to retrieve his cape, then he stops. He stands over me for a moment until he places a hand on the headboard above me and leans close. My heart skips a beat, and I can feel a new sweat break free down my back, but with him so close, I can almost see the man I am trying to remember.

The tension between us is thick and strained. I want to remember so desperately who Yonah is in the real world. I fight tears that swell as I raise my hand and place it on his cheek. He closes his eyes at my touch, and I say, "It's just like you said, the ones we were closest with are the hardest to remember. I want to remember him so badly." My voice cracks and Yonah opens his stirring eyes. "I can't remember him. I can't..."

Yonah reaches up and wipes my tears. "I hope that I'm him in your world." He presses his lips to my cheek, and I close my eyes to relish his touch. "Get some rest, my belle, there is still much for you to learn and do." He pulls away to stand, and in one fluid motion, he lifts the heavy cloak off me and drapes it around his shoulders. Yonah is mesmerizing enough to make me forget the chills that trickle up my frame when he pulls away his cloak.

Yonah heads for the door once his cloak is clasped. "I'll see you soon. Until then, be good to the Dais family, okay?"

Swallowing thickly, I give him a quick nod. "Okay."

His smile is gentle before he opens the door and leaves me to my thoughts. I'll have to figure out how to process everything Yonah has told me. If all of this is a dream, I still want to wake up. And if the only way to do that is to take Yonah's information seriously, then I'll do it...

Because I've realized I don't want to go home, I want to wake up to see him... whoever he is.

6

Dontaye

"Morning," Rachel says as I take a seat at the table. Charlie's father carved the table himself, apparently.

"Morning," I reply glumly. I've been lying in bed all week. Now that my fever has fled, I'm a little weak.

"You're finally out of bed." Rachel turns back to the cast iron skillet she has on the stove and flips the pancakes over. "You know I love you, sweet pea, but Christmas is coming, and we'll be needing some extra hands."

"Oh," I say. "Well, I guess it's only fair."

"Now, I don't want you to think of this as payment. You are part of this family." Rachel turns to me with a thick hand on her wide hip. "And families help and take care of each other. Besides, it's the Christmas season, darling." She waves her spatula around. "It's always the Christmas season here."

I frown. "Why?"

"Because we're always expecting the birth of Jesus."

I was going to ask why again, but I really didn't want to hear any religious nonsense so early. It's enough I had to fight the vexation I feel every time I hear the word *Christmas*, let alone, the annoyance of actually having to force myself to open up to God.

Better get comfy, I tell myself, *because I don't know when I'll ever open up to Him.*

A knock comes to the door and Charlie calls, "Can someone get that! Winter's got snow in her coat!"

"I told you not to take them out before breakfast!!" Rachel snaps back. Charlie goes silent, though I can hear Winny whining and Nite laughing in the living room where they remove their boots and coats. Charlie took the twins out to gather more firewood this morning and clearly got a little carried away with the fresh snow.

"I'll get the door," I tell Rachel as I move from the table. Following the wooden floor to the door, I reach up and open it to find Yonah smiling down at me.

"Oh," he says shyly. "Good morning, Belle. I wasn't expecting to see you this morning."

I squint. "Belle?"

"Yes. You're the Belle of The Native." He smirks and leans forward. "Or ... you're *my* belle." He winks as he stands erect. I gulp down some air that gets stuck in my chest. The pain is enough to make me cough, but I try to suppress it and let out smaller coughs, so the Guardian won't notice.

He doesn't and asks, "Well, can I come in or should I stay

out here?"

"No. Sorry." I clear my throat loudly. "Come in."

He strolls inside, passing me after he dries his feet on the carpet to head through the house. Yonah is head and shoulders over everyone, stronger and more handsome than anyone I've seen in The Native so far. His movements are elegant and regal, more princelike than Guardian. The way he politely greets Rachel only deepens my curiosity of him; he inclines his head and kisses her hand when she holds it out to him, like an old-fashioned gentleman. A barb of jealousy stabs me in the rear, and I shift my weight from one foot to the other as I watch the scene play out.

"Mrs. Dais, good morning," Yonah greets.

"YONAH!" Winny squeals before Rachel can answer. The little girl moves like lightning, crossing the kitchen to embrace the Guardian who takes a knee to hug her. She's still wearing her heavy coat, which is apparently filled with snow, but Yonah doesn't seem to mind.

He grins and says, "Good morning, Winter. How are you?"

"I'm good," she says shyly. Her eyes leave his, and the small girl blushes before the mighty Guardian.

He laughs at her shyness and pokes her nose. "I'm glad you're doing well today."

Winny can hardly contain herself as she bounces off in embarrassment to hide behind her brother. Nite has shaken the snow from his hair and found his place at the table already. He sits peacefully as he uses wax crayons to color a picture, only looking up to wave at the Guardian.

"Is that all I get, Mr. Aconite? A little wave for your favorite Guardian?"

Nite beams and sets his crayons down to run to Yonah. The small boy falls into his arms with glee, and Rachel laughs.

"Nite, be gentle. You'll knock Yonah over."

"No," Nite says as he holds onto Yonah. "Yonah's a Guardian, and he's the strongest person in the world."

Rachel laughs, but Charlie enters the kitchen and tuts, "Hold on, son, he's not stronger than your father!"

"Yes, he is!" Winny cries and runs from the table back to Yonah. The Guardian laughs as the twins hold on to either side of him.

"Alright," Yonah says to them, "let's see if I can lift you both?"

"At the same time?" Nite asks.

"Just you watch." He adjusts his grip on the two, and even Rachel stops cooking to enjoy the show. "Hang on," he says to the twins who squeal endlessly as they cling to the Guardian. Just before he stands, Yonah finds my eyes across the room and winks. With one push, he stands to his feet, lifting the twins off the floor and causing them to laugh in an endless frenzy.

"I can do the same!" Charlie exclaims like a wonderfully jealous father would.

"Now, now," Rachel crosses the kitchen to Charlie, "I know you're still strong. Ain't that enough?"

"Of course it is, sweetheart, but look at them," Charlie

64

complains. His brows fall low and his lips pout. "They love him."

"He's the Guardian, of course they do." Rachel says. "But they love you more, okay?"

Charlie sighs and nods, then he wraps a hand around Rachel's shoulders and says, "I guess you're right. Ain't nothing I can do about that. Even *I* love our Guardian."

I chuckle and Rachel leans back in laughter. The morning has only begun but it's off to a good start thanks to Yonah.

"Alright you two, I've got to put you down." Yonah lowers his voice. "Go run to your father, so he won't feel so bad."

"I heard that," Charlie calls.

Yonah laughs as he sets the twins down. They call for their Pa and run over to Charlie just as Yonah instructed.

"So…" Rachel sets plates on the table. "What brought you by?"

"I came to see if Charlie would be free next week for a Christmas round."

"You mean Saint Nicholas' trip?" Winter exclaims.

"That's right." Yonah nods.

Apparently, that's an exciting thing because Charlie and the twins are all thrilled. Rachel isn't but I still ask, "What's the Saint Nicholas trip?"

Rachel's brows jump to her hairline as she throws a dishtowel over her shoulder. "You've never experienced The Native's Christmas."

I shake my head.

"Every year, Yonah makes a trip around The Native to make sure everyone has supplies and all the help they'd possibly need to prepare for Christmas," Charlie explains as he lifts Nite to sit in his lap at the table.

"Oh, I see."

"It's a lot of fun," Charlie adds, "and I'm free whenever—"

Rachel clears her throat and turns around dramatically to give Charlie a dirty look. The fear in his heart comes out in stuttering words. "A-Actually, one of our h-horses just had a baby, while there's two goats waiting to give birth. I've got to be here for the goat births because our main lady has had complications in the past." Charlie sighs as he stands to swap places at the stove with Rachel. She takes a seat between Nite and Winter and adds, "We actually need the extra hands around here."

"No problem at all." Yonah inclines his head. "I've done them alone before, I just thought I'd offer since I know Charlie's been wanting to do one for a while."

Charlie only continues to sigh as he plates breakfast for us. Rachel and Charlie always swap places at mealtimes. Rachel does all the cooking since she's a better chef than Charlie, but he does all the serving, and they clean together at night. But Nite and Winter do the cleaning during the day.

There's silence in the house, just the sound of Charlie scraping the skillet. Yonah tries to remain hopeful, holding a tight smile, but I think he's a little disappointed. However, nothing gets by Rachel. She takes one glance around the room and lets out a deep breath. "Actually, Yonah, we really don't need all hands on deck."

"Please, Mrs. Dais, don't worry. It's no—"

"You know we're always willing to help," she says in a voice that only a mother could make. Somewhere between stern and concerned, whatever the case, Yonah is tightlipped and only nods in silent agreement with her. "So, I want you to take Taye along. It would be good for her to see The Native at its peak."

"I think that's a great idea!" Charlie perks up as he scoops eggs onto my plate.

"What? No, that's something special for you guys. Not me." I shake my head.

"Sweet pea, you are the 'you' in 'you guys' too. You're one of us until you go home. And even when you're home, you'll always be one of us. Not just a Dais." She pats her chest. "But a Native."

I try to think of a quick way to disagree, but Yonah turns to me and asks, "What do you think? You'll be in the safest hands possible with me, Belle."

That nickname makes me nervous, and I try not to react with everyone's eyes on me. I don't know how Yonah can just make up nicknames and not even feel slightly embarrassed to use them in front of others, but he doesn't seem to notice everyone's eyes on us.

"Well, I don't know. I've never—"

"She'll be going," Rachel assures Yonah and me both.

I look back down at my breakfast, cooling by the second,

as Yonah says, "Perfect. Pack for a week or so, and I'll be back in about five days for our trip."

"I'll have her ready," Rachel promises.

"Well then, I'll see you soon, Dontaye."

My real name catches my attention, but that's exactly what the Guardian wants. The corner of his mouth ticks up just slightly before he nods and bids the house farewell. I watch him as he turns away effortlessly. It's like he glides everywhere he goes, allowing his cloak to billow around him before it follows him out of the kitchen.

"Ezra!" Whitney called. She was a pretty girl, long blonde hair with eyes as blue as the ocean. She flounced over to Ezra and slipped her arms around his neck. "Hey," she said cheerfully. Ezra chuckled as he reached up to grab Whitney's arms.

"Hey," he said as he rocked to look over his shoulder at her. The two were "the cutest" couple at the university. I didn't think so, but Ezra seemed happy since he'd met her at the Christian club on campus. The two hit it off immediately, and lately I'd been seeing less and less of my *best* friend. I couldn't blame him, Whitney was perfect. She was pretty and *Christian*, what more could Ezra ask for?

Me… I wanted him to ask for me.

Why couldn't I just fake loving God? I didn't have to *actually* love Him; I could've cruised through church services and been happy with Ezra. Instead, I was stuck, sitting at the only campus table without an umbrella on the hottest day of the year, watching the one person I wanted to see happy, be happy without me.

"I better go," I said as I gathered my books.

"Why?" Ezra asked.

I was mid-reach when my eyes involuntarily snapped to Whitney who was still hanging around his shoulders like a child.

"Come on, Dontaye," Ezra strained, "don't go. We've barely finished anything."

"Yeah, well I can finish the rest inside where it's cool and easy to concentrate."

"Babe, let her go." Whitney's eyes flew to mine, and I could see in her what took Ezra two full years to see. At the time, I just thought it was my own bitterness and jealousy that was making her out to be a bad gal, unfortunately, it wasn't. "We can finish this up and then grab dinner."

Ezra looked apologetic for a split second before Whitney planted a kiss on his cheek. He brightened and agreed to her request. Of course he would, she was his girlfriend. I was just a friend who happened to be a girl.

"I'll see you around, Ezra," I said as I slung my pack over my shoulder.

He nodded but offered nothing more than that as he became totally enchanted by Whitney. Tossing her blonde hair over her shoulder, she talked loudly and laughed even louder, like the two of them were the happiest people on earth. They were ... for a little while at least.

After that day, Ezra and I didn't speak as much. Actually, we *stopped* speaking for the last six months of their relationship. The breakup was so bad, even I pitied him. But even after the breakup, I couldn't get myself to speak to him again. I didn't want to be the person who came running back because the door was open. Ezra was in a fragile state during that time, so I took things as they came. Smiles passed to each other in the hall, waves when he was up to it. Eventually, brief conversations about homework. It wasn't until we got partnered up in a general science class that we broke the ice. Literally.

"Crap!" I cried as the ice shattered to pieces on the floor.

"How'd you drop it?" Ezra snapped.

"I told you I don't have steady hands."

He rolled his eyes. "Of course you don't. Now we have to do this all over again." We were working after hours already because of me. I dropped the ice during the first trial in class. Our professor was kind enough to reserve the lab for us to finish after hours. But I kept dropping the ice.

"Well, here." I shoved the tongs into his chest. "You carry the stupid ice across the classroom."

"It's literally the one job you have. To just be steady. And you can't even do that."

"Me? Be *steady?*" I scoffed. "I tried, Ezra. But you're so busy with the entire world that you can't take the time to help me when I need it."

"Help you do what? Carry ice? Oh, sorry, let me help you every step of the way because you're incapable of doing anything on your own, but *I* have to do it all alone!"

I stared so long my eyes began to burn. Ezra shoved his hands to his face, and I said bitterly, "You don't get to blame me for Whitney."

"You weren't there for me!"

"And you left me!"

"I had a *girlfriend!*"

"So, I guess you didn't need me." I shrugged. "Not until you were too broken to fix yourself. *Now* you need me. Well, guess what? *I* don't need *you*." I snatched my folder from the table and hustled for the door when Ezra grabbed my arm to turn me to face him.

"Get off me!" I said harshly, but Ezra refused.

"Stop it," he demanded as I fought against him. "Stop!"

"No!" My voice cracked and the tears finally won the battle and began to fall. "I can't stop fighting you ... but I want to."

He struggled, opening his mouth twice but no words came out until his third attempt. "I was so blinded. So stupid. I couldn't make her happy because I couldn't ... I couldn't stop loving someone else..." his words fell short as he hung his head. With me pinned against the wall beneath his grip, I slowly freed a hand from his grasp to hug him.

We never found the words to say to each other. There was an empty space between us where all the unsaid words were thrown together. One day we'll figure out how to say the things we've always meant to say, but at least for that day, a gentle embrace was enough.

I gasp and spring forward. Blinking, I look around in the darkness, but the orange hue of the fire tells me that I'm still in The Native. But if I needed any more confirmation, Winter's snoring from our first day of chores together is enough. Sighing, I lay back in bed. I'd dreamt of someone and something painful. My hand finds my chest and I feel my heart thrashing within.

"It was him," I whisper to myself. The one I was dying to remember because he caused a storm of good and bad emotions. *I ... I miss him...*

I think.

7

Dontaye

Rachel and Winter packed me a satchel of supplies, along with some clothes and the only blanket they could spare. I'm grateful for what they've given me and hope to return soon to help with chores and decorations.

We—the Dais' and I—live in the forestry district. We're responsible for getting Christmas trees to all of The Native. Our district has the most livestock, so it was chosen long ago as the Christmas tree district because we have the mules to transfer the trees. That's why Rachel needs the extra hands. Charlie is better with the animals than Rachel is. He's delivered nearly every one of the goats we have, and three out of the six horses, not including the new one. He's needed here for that momma goat who's been having birthing complications. So, until that goat has her baby, Charlie will be home fixing the stables and sheering the sheep.

Rachel, on the other hand, will be working down in the carpenter's center. She has to help cut down trees and haul them onto trucks. That leaves the twins to take care of the house and me to run errands and work the market for us. But since I'm going on this trip with Yonah, the twins will be going to the market together while Charlie takes care of the house and the animals. It's a lot to cover, but Rachel assures me it's this busy every year, so the family will adjust to the workload the way they always do.

No one can stay to see me off. Rachel has to head to the carpenter's center while Charlie takes the twins down to the market to get them set up. So, I wait alone on the front porch for Yonah.

I frown as I dig my foot into the snow on the porch. Instead of playing with the snow, I should at least shovel this for them… it's the least I can do since I'll be off learning about the districts of The Native while they stay back and juggle a crazy workload for the season.

I grab Charlie's shovel, which he leaves on the side of the wraparound porch, then I begin digging into the thick layer of snow that'd fallen through the night. It's hard labor to shovel snow, usually Charlie does it alone. Some days he'll let Nite help, but Rachel, Winny, and I are always inside.

Wiping sweat from my brow, I huff out a white breath before beginning again. As I work from one side of the porch, I start to see the wooden logs piled against the house. I can feel myself smiling, though the blowing wind makes my face feel frozen. My arms burn, my back hurts, and my legs feel weak, but I don't want to stop. I want to do something for the people who have done so much for me. Shoveling snow won't amount to their kindness, but it's at least a start to express my gratitude.

"Who has the Belle of The Native working so hard so early?"

I turn to find Yonah standing there with a hand on his hip. He's wearing his uniform as always; a thick sweater, dark pants, shining black boats and his cloak. His dark hair is brushed back, showing off the angelic structure of his face, his divine radiance.

"Oh!" I wheeze. "I was just trying to do something before I left for the week." I sniffle deeply and realize, to my horror, that my nose is running. Sheer embarrassment forces me to respond. I drop the shovel and frantically wipe my nose and face before Yonah can get any closer.

"Don't wipe so hard." He laughs. "You'll hurt yourself."

"Can we go?" I brush by him and head down the stairs. Pulling my glove off, I try to fix my hair beneath my cap and pat my cheeks and nose to make sure everything is dry. Once I'm done, I shove my glove into the snow as an attempt to clean off whatever I wiped away from my nose, then I slip it back on before Yonah comes down the steps with my satchel.

"Is this all you brought?"

I nod.

"Well, there'll be markets all over. I'm certain you'll find plenty of things to buy there."

"Oh no," I throw my hand, "we didn't have any money to spare, so I'm just going along for the ride."

"Really?" Yonah tosses my bag into the back of the cart. He grabs a thick rope and ties my bag down and that's when I realize I didn't hear him, or his two chocolate brown horses arrive while I was shoveling.

"I've never done something like this before," I say dumbly. I can't remember if I have or haven't but, for the sake of not lapsing into depressing thoughts, I settle on believing I've never traveled through a country in just one week before.

"That's all the more reason to enjoy our trip to the fullest." Yonah comes over and smiles down at me. "I'll tell you what, if I find a coin behind your ear, that means this trip is on me. But if I don't, then you'll only be able to enjoy the adventure."

I can't help but laugh as I reach up and feel behind both of my ears like an amused little kid. "No coins there."

"Let me see." He reaches forward and feels behind my ear. "Ahh," he hums and retracts his hand with a single gold coin between his black leather gloved fingers. "There we go. I thought I saw something twinkling behind your ear earlier."

I scoff, but not indignantly, just in surprise. He flips the coin at me, and I catch it in my hands. I've only seen two gold coins up close and one silver coin since I've been here. We have a plethora of bronze coins at the house that Rachel and Charlie use regularly.

"No." I hold it out to him. "I can't accept anything from you, Yonah. I've got to start earning my own around here."

He nods slowly. "If that's how you feel. But you do know I'm the Guardian of The Native, right?" He places his wide hands on his chest and smirks as he leans down and whispers in my ear, "I've got all the gold I could need, so the world is yours if you say so." He steps back and offers me his hand. "Come on, beautiful, I want to show you as much of The Native as we can cover this week. I want to give you an adventure."

My cheeks are burning from trying to suppress the smile I'm hiding. I laugh and nod as I take his hand. "This is going to be a long week, isn't it?"

"But it'll be the best week of your life." He helps me into the cart. It has two compartments. A place for us to sit, and an empty wagon-like trunk with blankets all over, and safely attached to the back is our bags.

"Why's this part empty?" I ask as Yonah climbs into the cart to sit beside me. He gets the horses going before he answers, "That's where you'll be able to rest."

"And you?"

"I don't need much sleep."

I quirk a brow. "Don't tell me you're actually a guardian *angel?*"

He chuckles and glances over at me, up close, his princely features nearly stop my heart. "Not quite." He grins. It's blessedly gorgeous. "I've been blessed by God to be a Guardian, so there are certain perks to this job."

"Like no sleep? I can't imagine that as a perk. More like a crazy workload if it doesn't allow sleep."

Yonah laughs again. "You are secretly funny."

I shake my head as I smile at the winter wonderland. "No. Just painfully realistic."

"We'll see if I can get you to believe in God and The Native He built for you."

"In one week?" I ask.

"All things are possible with Christ." He bumps his shoulder with mine and I let out bright laughter that feels like a relief to let go of. It feels like I have been afraid to laugh all this time. But Yonah does something to me. He pulls my walls down and forces me to find the good and happiness in all of this world. No matter if it makes sense to me, Yonah's presence is enough to make me forget the confusion and just enjoy the moment.

We ride through the wintery world and Yonah points out different birds' nests in the trees. There's a winter owl Yonah shows me. I look for the owl, silently scanning until I spot his golden eyes blinking through the winter's grey. I yelp and scare it away. Yonah says there will be more to see than just owls resting through the day.

"Yonah," I call. He's leaning back, resting in the seat. He told me the horses knew the way, and we wouldn't have to worry about getting lost. When I asked if he was joking, he only smiled and leaned back to close his beautiful eyes.

"Yonah," I call again. His face is relaxed, and his long lashes are gently shut, shielding his bright eyes from the world. Looking at the Guardian while he's awake is hypnotic, but looking at him as he rests is mesmerizing.

I begin to fan myself as I glance around. Thick blades of the greenest grass I've ever seen are pushing up through the melting blanket of snow. Ice cracks beneath the hooves of the horses, and the wheels of the cart. The world changes before my very eyes, and I'm not sure what to do besides remove my jacket, hat, and gloves. The grey of winter is leaving, and the warmth of summer is finding its way into The Native as we travel along. The horses keep their stride, never breaking to acknowledge the wave of heat, but I break into a sweat and pull my jacket off.

"Yonah!" I shove him this time and he snorts. He grunts at the sunlight and shields his eyes as I sass, "I thought you didn't need sleep?"

"I don't, but it is nice to enjoy it every now and then."

I huff in annoyance as I roll my sleeves up. "Why is it getting warm?"

Yonah sits up and looks around. "We are very close to the heart of The Native."

"The heart? Like the *center* of The Native?"

"Yes. It's the oldest part of The Native where a small district of herbalists come from the earliest settlers of The Native."

"Settlers? How does this land have settlers if God created it for me in a *dream*?"

He smiles and nods. "Good question. Time doesn't exist here. So, the moment God decided to use your slumber as a spiritual reawakening, The Native was created. Rich with history and generations of people just for this moment."

"Basically, God created this place as if it's always been here. Like a parallel universe?"

"Almost, except The Native is special."

I tilt my head to the side. "How so?"

"You'll see." The Guardian pulls on the reins of the horses. "We'll stop here for the day."

I glance around. "In the middle of the forest?"

"It gets beautiful out here at night. The singing crickets and nature's song. A beautiful lullaby rings out to set the sun, and a melody continues through the night to bring rest to the weary."

Unsure of what to make of Yonah's sudden poetry, I choose to just nod along and follow his instructions to set up camp. Yonah asks me to unpack while he sets up a tent for me. It's quite lavish for a single night. Thick rope and long pegs, with sheep skin coverings that have wool attached to the inside as insulation. Yonah says the tent will be more useful once it gets cold again, but for now it'll be fine.

There isn't much for me to unpack from the cart. My bag, two bags of fresh vegetables, and other camping supplies. There are wrapped blankets and even a pair of mittens I'm sure wouldn't fit Yonah's hands.

"Yonah," I call over my shoulder. He yells back from the tent, and I ask, "Where are your things?"

"What do you mean?" His voice is close with my back turned. I turn around right into his sweaty chest and stumble back.

"Sorry," I mutter, peering up at him. He's... out of uniform. His normal dark sweater and cloak have been cast aside, now Yonah wears a white shirt and dark pants. He slings the hammer over his shoulder, so I get a good look at his corded biceps. Round lumps of flesh are molded into hard hunks of muscle. A vein runs from his wrist down his forearm. But there's another vein spindling across his round and bulky bicep that makes my eyes wander all over.

Tall with broad shoulders and a lifted chest. His core looks as strong and as firm as a tree trunk, with abs that are visible through his sweaty shirt. Yonah may wear a beautiful smile and bright flaring eyes, but he's formidable without a doubt. Now, I see why he's the Guardian.

"Sorry," I apologize again in the agonizing silence. When my eyes trace back up his frame, he's smirking at me.

"I'm not usually out of uniform, Belle, but if it'll catch your eye maybe I'll wear it less often."

Flustered, I turn back to the cart and fumble through it, trying to remember what I was even going on about before Yonah's stupid ripped body forced its way into my face.

Drawing blank, I sigh as I place my hands on the back of the cart. "Will I struggle to remember everything while I'm here?"

"No!" he calls loudly—from across the camp, all of a sudden. Just that quickly, Yonah has returned to setting up my tent. He steps out and yells to me, "You're just embarrassed, Belle! You'll remember when you calm down."

With everything in me, I fight the urge to roll my eyes.

8

The Guardian

I've only seen Dontaye's hair down once, and it was captivating. But tonight, when it's just the two of us, I'm free to enjoy her beauty like it's just for me. Mesmerizing mahogany curls fall over her slender frame. Dontaye is a small woman with light brown skin and wide babydoll eyes. She's beautiful beyond compare. I watch as she pushes a curl behind her ear with a delicate hand. Every move she makes, I want to see. It's like watching the rarest beauty perform right before your very eyes.

Dontaye's planted on a log with her slender legs reaching out just beneath the hem of her pink skirt. She's crossed her legs and bounces one as she reaches out to poke at the flames with a stick. The flickering orange light from the fire highlights her warm honey brown skin. It's hard to watch Dontaye most days. Seeing her grow stronger every day means our time grows shorter every day. However, as her Guardian and the Guardian of The Native, I'm forced to ignore the trouble in my heart. All I can do is be sure that Dontaye believes before it's too late. I have no worries about that because she's already changing.

When I saw Dontaye shoveling the snow, I knew her transformation had begun, and a heart of repentance wasn't too far behind. Her desires are changing. She's losing the desire to go home, and replacing it with gratitude, appreciation, recognition of the family around her. Recognition of someone's help in your life is the first step to salvation. If she can recognize her family's help, she'll soon come to recognize God's.

It's all just a matter of time. I've seen many hearts transform in my time here in The Native. Being honored as a Guardian comes with immeasurable perks. Beyond the gold and the gifts from the people, I am a protector and an instrument in the lives of those in The Native. God uses me to help many others, people who I thought were the assignment. However, as my last duty and final assignment, I can't be more honored to be working with Dontaye. She is special, and because of her, I am stronger than ever before.

I watch as Dontaye leans closer, peering into the fire as she tries to move a log that's too heavy for her little stick. I smile to myself and raise a hand. With the flick of my wrist, the flames obey my command and begin to dance for her. I keep my eyes on her the whole time. Watching her face change from concentrated to amazed. Her furrowed brows soften, and a gentle look of bafflement captures her features. Then fear sets in. She shakes her head a little and scoots back on the log. When her hand goes to her head and tears fill her eyes, I sink my hand to my lap and the flames stop.

"You weren't seeing things, Dontaye."

Her vision snaps to me and I give her a smile though I feel bad for making her think she's crazy. She's sensitive to conversations about her memory, but it's understandable. However, she's developed a fear of hallucinations now because of her struggles. The dreams she has are likely of her waking life. They're more vivid and realer than being here, but when she awakens the dreams are gone. So, when she sees things she's uncertain of, she feels panicked that she may be asleep.

"You saw those flames, too?"

I raise my chin. "I made them."

"What?"

"Come, I'll show you."

Dontaye hesitates. She moves slowly to come over to my log and sit beside me. I open my hand and lay it palm up on my leg. Dontaye watches intently as I wiggle my fingers. I can feel the heat within rushing through my body. It's looking for an outlet, so I command it to my hand and a flame bursts to life in my palm.

Dontaye gasps, but she doesn't move. "How... how are you doing that?"

"I'm a Guardian," I say. "I've been commissioned by God to protect The Native, therefore, He's blessed me with the gift of protection."

"How is fire the gift of protection?"

"The gift of protection is the Holy Spirit." I lift the flame. "This is His form as a flame, He has the form of wind, and the form of water. He doesn't have an earthen form because humans are created from dirt, and He is not human. He's a Spirit. But He can manipulate the earth because He did it before to create man."

"I don't understand any of this! Every day there's something new here!" Her eyes are filled with confusion as she pops to her feet.

"Wait," I say as I stand with the flame, "I don't want to scare you or confuse you. This is something special for Guardians. Everyone has the Holy Spirit, but we are given a double portion of faith to believe in Him for anything. That's part of being a Guardian, maintaining my faith." I look down at the flame. "Maintaining my belief that God can do anything through me."

When I look up, Dontaye's a little calmer. I take a chance and step towards her. She lets me enter her personal space and I ask her, "Do you trust me?"

Her shoulders bunch and I snort. "Little Belle, you'll have to trust me. I want you to feel the gentle yet raw power of God. He is a flame that you can get close to. He is the flame that can engulf you without burning you."

"How do I trust a man who isn't a man? How do I trust God?"

"I assure you, Belle, I am a man and when my time as a Guardian finishes, I will return to man as normal as Charlie. But right now, I have to be stronger for you."

"To protect me," she whispers as her eyes drop to the flame in my hand.

"Yes." I pause to speak softly. "Give me your hand."

Though fearful, Dontaye opens her small palm to me, and she has no idea that she's just taken another step in the righteous direction. Maybe she just wants to hold the fire in her hand, but she's going to encounter the flame of God's Spirit, hold *Him* in her hand. Or maybe, she really wants to see if God's power can be gentle and loving even as a hot, flickering flame.

Carefully, I offer her the flame as I place my other hand beneath her outstretched one. Her eyes bulge as the flame rests in her hand, speaking volumes to her belief in God.

"It's not burning me," she whispers. Her eyes change from frightened to joyful in an instant. Looking up from the flame, Dontaye beams with a smile. "It's not burning me! I'm holding fire!"

"You're holding the power of God."

Her eyes falter, and her smile fades. The wilted look holding her face captive almost convinces me that I was wrong about her progress... Almost.

"God," she says. "I know what He wants, I just don't know what *I* want."

"What do you—" I stop speaking when a chill runs down my spine. The air becomes stiff with emptiness, and the chirping crickets are suddenly silent.

"Are you alright?" Dontaye asks as she looks up at me. She pouts as she begins to tremble. "It's getting cold."

"Focus on the flame." I turn away for my sweater and cloak. I pull on my sweater first and then throw the heavy cape around my shoulders, letting it clasp in place on its own. "Stay quiet, and stay behind me," I say, walking back to Dontaye, "and don't stop focusing on that flame. Protect it no matter what."

She looks worried but asks no questions, thankfully. She produces a nod which is good enough for me. I move to stand in front of her to watch for what I know is to come.

The midnight song has stopped and the new melody that begins comes from the voice of small children somewhere in the distance. As they move closer, the singing doesn't get louder, it gets chaotic. Like they suddenly can't remember the words to their own song, like they've forgotten how to use their voices. It's like their ears become deaf and their mouths become mute, yet they force out a song as if they are singing somewhere below a pit of water. There's terror in their voices, distorted fear. The cheerfulness and innocence of a child defiled. The song could confuse a weak person, but Dontaye's holding on to the flame of the Holy Spirit, so I know that she'll be fine.

"What's that noise!?" Dontaye screams out.

I whip my head to see her falling to her knees, cradling the flame against her chest.

In Hebrew, I whisper, "Jesus, consume her."

The flame cries aloud and stretches its fiery hands to envelope Dontaye as she shivers on the ground. When I look back, the singing creatures have arrived. The trees rustle with their madness, and the shrubs shimmy from their intrusion.

"Guardian," a raspy voice calls from the bushes.

He's hiding.

"You know that anyone who does not believe is due to us."

"She is due her fair chance to believe," I say firmly. "You will honor the code and take your leave now."

"She has had her fair chance," the raspy voice snaps. "Give her to us!" The voices cry along with the first voice, calling me to give Dontaye to them. "It is our season for compensation! Give her to us so we may have her flesh and drag her to our home!"

"You will not have her," I say sternly as I remove one of my gloves. I reach down and touch the earth. "From dust you shall come, and from dust you shall return." I stand and slip my glove back onto my hand. "You do not wish to do this here."

"This is our land—"

"You own no land here!" I yell back. I'd planned to reveal more of a Guardian's true form to Dontaye over time, but today, she'll have to take it all in at once.

I glance back at Dontaye whose eyes are bulging as she blinks through the fire. I'll have a mountain of explaining to do when all this is over. I give her my best smile before dropping it to turn back to the creatures hiding in the dark. "You've given me no choice," I say darkly.

"We are not afraid, because we are not alone." The voices speak in unison, "You are but one Guardian, we are Legion;

for we are many." The voices echo through the forest before a shriek shreds through the bushes and the voices go silent.

"Here we come."

As quickly as the distorted voices speak together is as quickly as the small and round devils break out from the bushes and trees. They come from above and from all around. Their sharpened teeth for eating flesh, and their pointed fingers for scratching and tearing at their opponents. They are ugly dark creatures with pointed ears and humped backs despite being no taller than a toddle. Venom drips from their open mouths as they run at me, howling and screeching in madness to confuse me, but God is not the author of confusion.

"Rise!" I call to the ground.

At my command, the earth obeys, and soldiers made of dirt and stone rise from the ground. The figures are packed with hard minerals that lie deep within the earth, and they erupt like an army charging forward to crush the small creatures. I watch as the dirt warriors fight fiercely. Each time one is beaten, it crumbles to dirt, just to rise again. The dirt men throw themselves at the little creatures, and even the trees come to life. They wave their branches wildly and shake their leaves violently to swarm the creatures and bat them away from the battle. They do this because the little elves are not the real enemy. They are the distraction.

The real enemy is lying in wait. With the earth fighting his minions and shoving him out of hiding, he's forced to come face to face with me.

Heavy hooves pound into the dirt, taking one long step at

a time. I wait as the man-beast moves through the battlefield to stand before me. Sharp horns jut from his head, and his face is distorted between man and beast. He has the face of a goat, yet when you look at him, he still seems to look human. Like a face is painted over his goat features. He bears a man's naked chest and arms, though today he's decided to wear his red coat. He doesn't wear pants; just lets his hairy grey goat legs move freely.

"Well," his voice is inhuman and grating. It sounds of a lost man somewhere in his chest, fighting against the voice of a goat. As if the goat has learned to talk through its bleating banter while wrestling with the human inside. "Guardian," he hisses as he mocks me with a bow. He raises his head and his rectangular goat eyes hold a menacing look in them. One of them begins to wander, splitting his vision to keep an eye on me and watch Dontaye just off to my right. His eyes brighten at the sight of her, and his wandering eye slams back into focus on me.

"Give her to me," he says quickly. His jaw drops open and acid drains from his mouth, burning the ground as the black goop touches it. His snakelike tongue comes out and he tries to hold a smile the best a goat can. "Give her to me!"

"She is not yours, Krampus, and you know it."

"She is not *His* either, so she must belong to someone. To ME!" he says giddily. "Me!" He jumps and clicks his hooves together. "Me! Me! Me!" His voice turns from giddiness to a monstrous sound. Rasping through his words, his screaming grows bleating as he husks out one last, "Me!"

I don't move. I have to wait and focus. Krampus is fast and plays the fool, giving him the capabilities to trick you if you aren't focused. I can't even look back at Dontaye. Breaking my gaze for a second is all he needs. It's how he gets children and drags them away year after year. When a parent's focus is lost even for a second, their child becomes defenseless, and Krampus is able to manipulate that child or simply yank them from their parents' grasp.

"Fine," his head twitches and then snaps to the side. "You will not give her. Then I will take her." He steps forward and moves around the flame, crossing one foot over the other. I follow him with my eyes until he stops abruptly. "You are good, Guardian, better than the rest I've fought." He raises his clawed fingers. "Let's turn out the light." With a big breath, he spews his acidic saliva into the firepit, and the flames die immediately, leaving us in darkness... but not total darkness.

Dontaye hollers out in fear within her flame encasement. It's the only light in the forest now, and it's all I need. The light from God cannot be extinguished.

Krampus heaves and jerks forward, running on just his goat legs, but he drops down to all four, digging his human hands into the ground to haul himself forward.

Shoving an arm through the air, I direct the wind to hurl into Krampus, knocking him off his footing and sending him tumbling into the ground.

"Coffin!" I scream.

Tree roots burst from the ground and slam themselves around Krampus. They tighten around him as he begins to spew his acid. The roots shrivel immediately, and his coffin begins to open, setting him free.

"Get up!" I yell as I run to Dontaye. She's screaming in panic on the ground, engulfed in the flames of God. I reach down and pull her to her feet as she cries hysterically. I take a breath and glance around; I'd taken my eyes off Krampus when I knew I shouldn't. Dontaye's cries stop suddenly, and when I look back down at her, she smirks. Her head snaps back and horns push through her mouth, and then his hands follow as Krampus shoves his way out of the illusion.

"Brazen Rain!" I call to the clouds as I push a cackling Krampus away. Thunder coughs and lightning hurls itself to the ground, crackling along the earth to light the path to Dontaye. Shards of rain flood down, twisting like thrown daggers at Krampus. The goat man runs like fire, dodging the shards and skipping out of the way. I jog along the path of light, searching for Dontaye while checking on the rain. Krampus is still fighting it, dodging the shards that are following him.

"Get away!" I come to a stop when the lightning path ends and Dontaye is at the end of it, fighting and kicking at the elves who try to touch her. Four lay dead around her, singed from attempting to touch the flames of God.

"Dontaye, come to me!" I call.

When I turn back, Krampus is racing towards me, faster than I can dodge. Lifting my hands, I slam my forearms together and the material of my sweater comes together to create a shield. It hardens in time as Krampus throws a punch, sending me stumbling backward, breaking the shield in two. I dodge Krampus's hits and punches with each arm shield, then I dig my feet into the ground and lock the shield into place and call again, "Rise!" More dirt men burst from the earth, and one erupts right beneath Krampus, sending him falling backwards. In those seconds of Krampus falling off balance, I use every single one of them to my advantage.

Clasping my hands together, I pray for the Sword of the Spirit. I whisk my hands apart as far as my wingspan will allow, the sword grows in my hands. Snatching it out the air, I swipe at Krampus who's beating through the dirt men. He falls forward on his hands and gives a mighty kick to three dirt men with one of his goat legs. One of the dirt men hurtles into four others and they all explode into dirt again. Before they can rise, he jumps atop the dirt piles and stomps all over them with his heels.

With his back turned, I swipe at him again, this time landing a blow to his back. He hollers, whirling around to thrash at me. I jump back, and he spits his acidic saliva, but I manage to raise a shielded arm, so the acid clings to my shield and singes it off.

Slamming the sword into the ground, I thrust my hands onto either side of it. "The Potter's Coffin!" Red clay bursts from the ground in big walls all around Krampus. The man-beast looks petrified as he lunges forward to escape, but the trees beside us join the battle and grab him, dragging him back to his coffin the way he's done children for years.

With my palms face up, I slap my hands together quickly,

and the clay erupts at the command. Crashing together, the clay encloses Krampus, and the goat man begins to scream from inside.

"Father! Hear my prayer for a flame!" With outstretched hands, I call to God for the flames that burn before the Lord on His throne. "Rain of flames, dance and fight. Cast your roaring fire and imprison him tonight."

God hears my plea and sends His fire. A pillar of fire bursts from the clouds and streams right down onto the clay coffin, making the clay hard and solid as rock.

Turning away, I grab Dontaye by the hand as she screams, and I pull her into my chest. Inhaling deeply, I force all the air from my lungs on the exhale. My cloak splits and thrusts out on either side of me and forms large black wings that stretch wide. With a mighty flap of my wings, I soar into the air and fly away from the dark scene to find winter again.

9

Dontaye

The sun is bright, reaching through the windows to wake me. I squeeze my eyes to block out the light as I pull the blankets back. They're heavy, weighed down like someone has rested a pile of bricks on top of me. I sit up and stare at the black cloak placed over my blankets. The memories from last night come back in a violent storm. The frightening images of the goat man named Krampus, and the little elves who tried to drag me away darken my mind's eye.

"The fire," I whisper.

I remember when Yonah passed me the flame and then he said something that made the whole thing engulf me. But I wasn't burned at all. Only the elves were burned when they tried to touch me. The flames were protecting me. I reach out and touch the Guardian's cloak, and shock zips through me, bringing back the last memory I had before passing out in shock. It was the Guardian's cloak whipping open like wings and flying through the air.

"Yonah," I say to myself.

"Good morning," he replies from the corner of the room.

I yelp and jump at the sight of him as he stands from the chair to come over to me.

"How are you?" He reaches forward to touch me, but I inch away from him. He sighs and drops his hand to his side. "Belle—"

"My name is Dontaye," I snap. What happened last night is freaking me out and I'm angry because I'm confused and still somewhat scared while the pieces are coming together.

"Dontaye," he says calmly. "Look at me."

I refuse, but he says it again, "Look at me."

I look up at him, and he gently places a gloved hand beneath my chin. "You are even more beautiful in your anger and confusion. But I will not keep anything from you today."

"Then tell me something because I feel like I'm losing my mind again." My voice cracks. "What happened last night? Who is Krampus and why can you do the things you can do?"

I can tell he pities me as he looks at me. His tender bright eyes are easy on me, and I brace myself for the truth.

"I am a Guardian," he says, still holding my chin. "And as a Guardian, we have special powers given to us by God. Not just to protect The Native, but to protect those whom we're assigned to."

I lick my lips. "Are you assigned to me?"

"I am. Because I am a reflection of someone in your

waking life who prays for you. Someone whose prayers have been protecting you all along."

"I don't understand. I thought The Native was created specifically for me. How could there be other Guardians assigned to other people?"

He finally releases my chin and steps back. "The Native was created for you, this means it is allowed to experience history, and it changes so you'll be able to recognize this place as a world, not just a dream land."

"So, if this world is for me, then what was that last night? What does that have to do with me?"

"You mean Krampus? That's his name in this world. But it's different in yours. And his purpose is different in your world. Here in The Native, Krampus preys on children in the hopes of getting his hands on baby Jesus. So he can end Him."

"But what's his goal in *my* world? What's his real name?"

The Guardian shies away from the question. "That's not something for me to discuss. But I can tell you he's an evil spiritual being, and those elves are the children he's dragged to torment. The children are released from their torment and turned into those little elves when Krampus needs their help."

"So, Krampus is an evil spirit that comes here to hunt children in the hopes of catching Baby Jesus... so why is he after me and not Baby Jesus?"

"Like I said, Krampus is The Native's version of a spirit that is hunting you in the real world. It's replicated here so you can understand not just God's love but also His secret protection." Yonah pauses like he's making sure I'm still following along. After a moment of silence, he says, "Evil spirits are never successful when they try to hunt those in the light."

"But I'm not in the light."

Yonah shakes his head. "You are learning, but last night you *were* in the light. Remember when you were encased in those flames?"

"I do," I say, thinking about the fire that surrounded me.

"Krampus can't fight the light, though he always tries. But last night was more of a permanent thing."

I squint. "Permanent?"

Yonah nods. "Krampus will never return because his time here has ended. Our battle was always destined because someone in the real world has fought this same battle for you. And since I am of the light, I knew I would win. He hoped *he* would win."

"Does that mean, all this time," I pause to piece my thoughts together, "he's dragged children away to torment while he waited for me? If you're my Guardian, and you were always destined to fight him and he came for me, that means he's been waiting for me, right?"

"Yes, but only because Krampus doesn't believe in second chances the way God does. He thought that since you hadn't accepted Christ yet, then you never would in the future. So, he came for you." He moves his shoulders slightly as he speaks quietly, "Don't feel bad or rushed because of what Krampus used to do. God has a timeline that no one can break, even those who exist outside of time."

"So, why wouldn't He just send me earlier so no one would have to die because of me?" I slam a hand to my chest, but Yonah remains calm.

Crossing his strong arms, he asks, "Is it fair that no one should be tested or tried? Only the ones who exist when you are here?" He pauses, but I have no answer. "Well, then everyone in the Old Testament would have been wrongly judged because they existed *before* the Savior was born. But God is fair and just, and He gave man free will from the beginning of time. Man had the freedom to choose righteousness and unrighteousness even in the Old Testament."

I throw my hands up in frustration. "*Humans* have free will! Not spiritual beings!"

Yonah raises a dark brow and looks me over. He's absolutely patronizing in the thick silence. I feel like exploding, but Yonah ignores my frustration and speaks coolly to me. "I've told you; we are people you'll meet or have already met. We are spiritual representations because man at his core is a spirit being wrapped in flesh."

A chill rolls down my spine in the silence. Not the chill that comes when you're frightened, the kind that cools your frustrated anger. There isn't anything left to say, nothing left to argue or fight against. Those who've been dragged away still had free will because everyone is actually a spirit being.

"Angels and Lucifer had free will first, yet they chose different. Your world has Satan and demons who try to trick people and cause illusions just like Krampus has done with his elves here."

I shake my head as I say softly, "I can't save the world, but I can save the people here in The Native if I stop fighting God."

"You must learn at your own pace, Belle. Don't rush yourself or force yourself to believe. Learning about God and who He is at your own pace makes this a love story."

"That's the thing…" I look up as I grip the fuzzy blankets. "When I was wrapped in those flames last night, I felt loved for the first time in my entire life. I know I can't remember anything from the real world, but this is something I'm certain of. I have never been loved before."

"But that raw and gentle power made you feel His presence, His love, *real* love for the first time."

I nod. "I … I don't want to admit that I want to feel loved again. I was afraid of Krampus, but I didn't have to be. I knew I was protected with those flames, and I knew even though I didn't understand it all, Jesus loves me." I take a breath to fight the tears. "Why does He love me so freely?"

Yonah reaches over and grabs one of my hands. "That's the best thing about Jesus. He loves for nothing in return. He loves because He *is* love and we are His."

Swallowing thickly, I can still feel myself deep within resisting the love of God, but it is admittedly getting harder to keep that up after last night. My confusion and unworthiness make me feel guilty and ashamed for not believing earlier.

"I want to let it all go and I want to make an effort to believe in Him if it will help The Native."

"And you? Do you want to believe for yourself?"

I know answering this will break down the walls inside, so I wait to answer. I need to know if this is for me. For a second, it truly isn't, it's just for The Native. But I remember Yonah said things here will affect me in the real world. I'll be better prepared for life after this. So I answer, "Yes. I want to believe in God for myself. For the me who will wake up one day and realize just how much God went through to save me."

Yonah wraps an arm around me and whispers, "I'm so proud of you, Dontaye."

"Thank you for protecting me last night."

He leans back and smiles down at me. "You are my Belle; I will protect you with my life." A sheepish grin washes over me, and Yonah pulls me close to peck the top of my head. "Get some more rest. I'll come back with lunch when you're better rested."

When I wake up, there's jellied toast and warm milk sitting on a silver tray on a wooden stool by my bed. I scarf down the toast and guzzle the milk, which gives me milk burps for five minutes straight. When that ordeal is over and I freshen up with the pale of water left for me, I leave the room which seemed so much smaller when Yonah was in it with me.

"You must be Dontaye." A beautiful woman the color of nutmeg sits at a table winding yarn around a small carousel. Her fingers move gracefully, pulling and twisting the scarlet yarn that resembles her own scarlet hair. Tresses of red flow

101

down to the floor like a carmine river running down her back. She's a tall woman, I can tell just from her height in her seat. When she turns to me, I can see her gentle, calm face and her extraordinary eyes.

I gasp when I see them. They are red too, bright red, with auburn lashes and brows.

"I-I am," I finally manage to speak but I can't say any more than that.

The woman laughs. "Do I frighten you?"

I shake my head. "No, I've just never—"

"Met a member from the Bleeding-Heart District?"

I shrug slowly, trying to figure out if she means she's from the Bleeding-Heart District and happens to be here, or that this is the Bleeding-Heart District, and *I* happen to be here. Regardless, the conclusion is that people from the Bleeding Heart are tall, red-headed people with brown skin and mystifying eyes.

"Right," I answer.

"Well, that's alright. We do not leave our district very often. The work we do in preparation for Christmas requires all hands on deck all year round."

"You prep for Christmas all year?"

She nods, glancing up from her threading. "All the districts do, except the Forestry District. But only because raising cattle and growing trees helps all of us year-round. They are integral to our Christmas celebrations, but their work is common work."

"I see. Because it's not specifically for Christmas."

"Precisely." She smiles, and I spot her pointed fangs. I look off, hoping she doesn't see me staring, but her calm voice comes, "We are vegetarians—if you can believe it. Our fangs are for scaring off the little elves that pass through."

"Elves? Like the ones with Krampus?"

She stops her carousel. "You've met Krampus?"

I lean forward. "I have. But Yonah did something to him last night." She arches a red brow, and I go on. "He placed him in a—"

"Belle, the new beauty of The Native meets my first love." Yonah walks inside, dusting the snow from his dark hair. His eyes meet mine briefly before shifting to the red-headed woman—apparently, the Guardian's first love.

"Well, well, I see that you have kept to my guidance, Guardian, and you have stayed within the measures from last year," she says as she stands from the chair.

"I didn't want to disappoint you." Yonah smirks and crosses the room, that's when I notice his clothes have changed. He's wearing blue pants with thin red stripes tucked into leather boots with a silver buckle. His typical dark sweater and black cape have been replaced with a deep red vest over a crisp white shirt, and a long military style jacket made of navy-blue velvet with yellow tassels on each shoulder to top it off. The crisp white shirt beneath the jacket and vest is open, and the navy-blue coat reaches the floor to make the Guardian look like a well-dressed prince and not the defender of The Native.

Still sporting leather gloves, except these have a silver button, Yonah reaches out and brushes away a lock of hair from the woman's shoulder. She brightens as he stands just an inch over her. "I have missed you, Nikolas," she says lustfully. Her eyes become half-lidded as Yonah's hand reaches her neck. She oozes all kinds of emotions at his touch while Yonah only watches her melt at his grasp. I suddenly feel like I'm watching something I shouldn't be, but Yonah's unwavering reaction is the only reason I stay.

"It has been quite a while, my love, but I am here," Yonah says. He leans forward and kisses her cheek. I don't know what's going on anymore. I just stand there, glued to the floor in shock.

Initially I thought this was one-sided until Yonah called her "love" and kissed her cheek. Now I feel like I'm watching two people fight with everything in them not to fall onto the table behind them and make love.

Who is she to Yonah? Is she really his first love? I bite my lip harder than I mean to, and the taste of blood rushes over my tongue. Slipping a hand to my lip, I sigh when I pull it away and spot the red on my finger. *Why do I feel so frustrated?*

"Belle," Yonah calls to me. He turns and offers me his hand. "I want you to meet my first love, Faraine, but we call her, Faire."

I hesitate when I look at his gloved hand. Ignoring the frustration, I take his hand and he places my hand in Faire's hand. "Faire, meet my Belle, Dontaye."

"We've met." Faire nods. "But it is a pleasure still."

"Yes, it is."

"Faire was the woman I fell in love with long ago. She

took care of me after I was injured during a trip through The Native."

"He was injured fighting a swarm of elves who were claiming that we owed them," she corrects. "I found Nikolas lying in the snow." Her eyes become empty as her mind travels to a distant memory. "He was lying there with a broken wing and so I took him and helped him."

"When you say Nikolas, do you mean Yonah?" I ask as she lets my hand go.

"Yes, pardon me, that is the name I gave him when he awakened."

"You *named* him?"

"She did." Yonah laughs. "I woke up and everyone here was calling me Nikolas, I thought for a second my name actually *was* Nikolas. However, Faraine named me because I'd been out for two weeks and whenever someone asked about me, she told them that was my name."

"He needed a good name." She smiles. "Nikolas in our mother tongue means *victory of the people*. He's like a saint to us."

Saint Nikolas... I feel even more mystified as I ask, "He won a battle for you?"

Instead of answering, Faire grabs my hand and leads me through the beautiful home. Stone floors that don't creak like the wooden ones from the Dais's cabin. Brick interior and large furniture made of leather. The Bleeding-Heart District seems to be well-off compared to the Forestry District.

Faire brings me to a fireplace, wide and tall with a flame burning within the hollowed wall. Above it hangs four red and white stockings. But above the fireplace is a painting. It's a woman shedding tears in the middle of snowy land laced with blood.

"Krampus comes for those who do not believe in Jesus," Faire begins to explain, "and back then, he came for one of us. One of us who'd taken chance after chance for granted to make things right with God. They were owed, but Nikolas came and extended a peace offering to the elves. When they wouldn't take it, an all-out battle began." She stops to shift her gaze to the painting, and she reaches up to touch it. "The Guardian almost lost his life fighting to protect one child who was not innocent. He was not as strong as he is now." She laughs to herself. "Yet he fought with everything in him and sent the elves and their darkness home."

"The girl, is she still here? Does she believe in God now?"

Faire's eyes find mine as she turns to me with a stiff smile. "She believes more than anyone here. It's why she became the Bleeding-Heart of this district." She turns away and heads through the rest of the house, leading me to a tall door. When she opens it, the wind rushes in and I throw my arms around myself. "The one crowned the Bleeding-Heart means they are the one whose heart was broken beyond repair. It will bleed into the streets, telling everyone of the goodness of being broken." Faire turns back to me as the winter's wind whips through her red hair. "The goodness of being liberated."

"I don't understand, how is being broken being liberated?"

"God works with broken pieces. If you are broken beyond

repair, that means God will never stop working on you. Of course," she laughs, "nothing is beyond God's repair, but only a great leader can remain humbled by their brokenness to allow God's Hand to fix the things they cannot."

Rubbing my arms, I nod. "But what does the cold have to do with this?"

"Ahh…" She turns, sweeping her hand across the ledge of the house she stands on. "The district is here, come have a look."

"It's so cold," I say through short breaths. My eyes bulge at her toned arms free of coverings and her strong legs free of pants, her bare feet standing in the snow. All she wears is a red top with thin straps, and a loin cloth that sweeps down to the ground.

"I cannot feel the cold," she says as she touches me. The wind continues, but I can no longer feel the coolness of it anymore. The snow falls, but it doesn't bring me any shivers at her touch.

Nervously, I step out onto the ledge of the house to look out at the district. There are streaks of red running through the clean white snow while people who look just like Faire work in groups. Some are picking plants, others are chopping them. There are buildings I can't look directly into, but there are tents I can see inside. Children and adults take turns stomping inside of buckets.

"What's that?" I point to the tents. The red streaks are all coming from the tents.

"That is where we crush the blood root. It is what gives

107

our stockings their color."

"The blood root?"

"Yes. The stockings." She points to a building. "They are made there. Hundreds and thousands are made all year round for Christmas; to deliver to the other districts."

"You guys make *stockings* all year?"

"We do." She turns and reenters the house. "Originally, we delivered red paint every year, but after Nikolas, we began delivering stockings as a symbol of our appreciation."

"How are stockings appreciation?" I ask as we come back to the fireplace.

"When Nikolas first arrived, he offered gold to the elves, but they didn't want it. The satchel was ripped in the fight, but when it was over, every coin was collected and returned to Nikolas." Her smile becomes as warm as the fireplace as she recalls the fond memories. "When he awakened, the one he saved only had that stocking full of his coins to give him as an offering of gratitude. But he didn't keep it. Instead, he left through the night, and placed a gold coin in every stocking in every house of our district."

Reaching out, I touch one of the stockings hanging above the fireplace. It's warm from the heat of the flames. "That's what you were threading in there? Another stocking?"

"Yes. We dye our yarn from the blood root plant and spend countless hours making countless stockings for The Native. It is our contribution to the celebration of our Jesus."

"But don't you remember Yonah through these stockings?"

She shakes her head. "We may remember Nikolas, but these stockings are symbolic of our remembrance of God's saving grace that day. He sent the Guardian to save our district from an elf invasion." She pauses. "God sent the Guardian to save the one lost sheep of the ninety-nine. One small girl…" Her breath becomes short as she places a hand on her chest. A single tear runs down her cheek as she says, "I was the one small girl. I was the lost sheep."

10

Dontaye

"You saved Faire," I say as I pack my things into my satchel.

Yonah leans against the wall in the corner of the room, watching me but not speaking.

"Is that why she was your first love?"

"She was the first person I ever risked my life for. The first person I impacted. I think love is a rather strong word, but appreciation isn't strong *enough*."

I nod as I fold a shirt. "How long have you been a Guardian?"

"For centuries. Time is different here, like I said."

"Centuries." I look over my shoulder at him. "You've been alive for centuries?"

He pushes off the wall and comes over to me. Leaning over me, his eyes focus not just on my face but on my very presence, like I'm the only person in the world he wants to see.

"I've been waiting centuries for you."

My mouth goes dry. All I can do is stare at the Guardian. He looks emotional, like he meant every word he just said, which makes me steam with nerves. I want him to mean what he's saying, but that's stupid. He's a Guardian. I'm just asleep. *When I wake up, he'll forget me and find a new Belle.*

"I should finish packing." I look back down at my bag.

"Hey," he whispers. He lowers himself beside me into my line of vision. "I don't want to scare you away, but there will be many people you'll have to meet with similar stories. I love them all." He pauses and I take a moment to blink away the stinging in my heart. "I love all of The Native because I am its Guardian. But you are special to me, Dontaye. You never have to worry about that."

"I don't want to be special," I say quickly. "I want to go home, remember?" Those are the words I want to hear, but I can't stop the pain in my chest. I want him to really mean what he said to me, not just tell me sweet words because I'm upset. He *could* mean them … but I won't let my heart take that chance. I can't even look at him as my ears burn. I hold on to the shirt in my hand as he stays close for another moment. I thought his unwavering determination would keep him there so I could apologize, but it doesn't.

"How could I forget?" he says before he stands and leaves the room.

Shoving the shirt into my lap, I grit my teeth as I hold in a cry. I want to scream and tell Yonah I didn't mean it, but what does it matter? I am only dreaming, and I can't forget that. Besides, the special girl falling in love with her Guardian is a tale as old as time, and time doesn't apply here.

I stand and shove everything off my bed and onto the floor. My brain is too foggy to be thinking of love, to develop feelings in such a short amount of time. None of this makes sense. Not to mention Faire's story of how she rejected God for so long that the elves came for her. They'd done the same for me. She almost lost her district; my lack of faith could make *all* of The Native crumble. I don't have time to try to love anyone, I have to learn to love God.

Rolling over, I climb out of bed and kneel beside it. With my hands clasped and eyes closed, I take a deep breath. "God, I don't understand my own anger towards you, but whatever it is in my waking life, help me to get over it. Help me now, God, so that The Native will be saved. In Jesus' name, amen."

I sit there a while, wondering if my prayer reached God, wondering if I'd even prayed correctly.

When morning arrives, Faire and a fleet of red-headed men and women wave Yonah and I off for the rest of our trip. Which is unbearable. We sit in the cold cart, bumbling along as the horses trot, without speaking a word. I don't even know how Yonah got our horses and belongings from the forest where we left Krampus, but I saw him whispering to the horses before we left today, and I think that's why we haven't stopped. Yonah has special powers, maybe he whispered a prayer to keep their legs moving and their bellies full.

In the insufferable silence, I ache. I just want to tell Yonah that I'm sorry. I was only frustrated for a stupid reason. A reason I can't really even name. My eyes drift to his profile in the quiet of our travel. The snow crunches beneath the heavy horse hooves, and the branches of low hanging trees rustle against our cart when we pass them. Winter's silence is eerie, but it hasn't been unbearable until now.

God, I'm praying because I don't know what else to do. I want to say something to Yonah. I want to apologize, but it feels so awkward. What do I do? I ask in the name of Jesus, amen.

God doesn't answer, but I don't think He needs to. I know pushing Yonah away when he isn't trying to hurt me isn't right. It's why I prayed last night and just prayed again. It only makes sense for me to be special to Yonah anyway; he *is* my Guardian. I'm the one making things awkward, and I shouldn't. All I have to do is apologize and make it clear that I know Yonah doesn't really like me, and I don't like him. We are Guardian and traveler, nothing more… at least that's what I'm going to tell him.

Before I can drift down another road of confusion, I huff away the thoughts of 'something more' with my Guardian. Sucking it all up and leaning into the feeling in my belly to apologize, I finally say into the silence, "Yonah, I'm sorry about last night. I shouldn't have said that. I was just feeling… frustrated."

"You were feeling afraid," he says.

I take a peek at him, and he's still looking ahead at the horses.

"Afraid to love in a world you'll forget. But to me," he looks at me and I feel my heart surge, "that's the best place to love."

"I'm not afraid that I'll forget you." I look at my hands. "I'm afraid you'll forget me."

"You are truly precious, Belle." Yonah grabs my hand and kisses it, stirring a flame of nerves within me. I snatch my hand away which makes him chuckle as he says, "You are certain that you won't forget me, but you're not certain that I won't forget you. I'm your Guardian, Belle. When you leave, I'll just be serving The Native, not one person. So," he reaches for my hand again, "I'll never forget you."

"Oh," I whisper shakily.

"You don't have to love." He laughs. "But promise me you won't try to fight your feelings. In this world, you're supposed to feel and experience everything you possibly can. That's what dreams are made for."

"To experience everything." I pause and look at my hand in his. "Even love?"

"It may seem sudden, but time is not the same here. Your heart can change faster than the blink of an eye here. So, it's okay to love."

I sit quietly for a moment, just blinking at our hands. Is Yonah telling me that he loves me, and he wants me to love him back? Or is he just helping me?

Faire really frustrated me with her closeness to Yonah, though I know it's more of a young girl's undying admiration and gratitude. But that shouldn't have frustrated me. I shouldn't feel things like this for Yonah. He's my Guardian. Not just some guy you fall for... but that doesn't cast aside the way he makes me feel. The way his gentleness has pushed me to seek God. Last night I issued my first prayer because of him. This morning, I issued a second because of him. Maybe problems are meant to bring us to God, not push us away from Him.

Suddenly, the horses slow and Yonah steps out of the carriage. He helps me out and we move through the snow to the mountain's edge.

"Do you see down there?"

Gripping my Guardian for dear life, I peek over the edge with every intention of running away out of fear, but the beauty below freezes me. A chilling grey world with equally grey people. But they are the most beautiful people I've ever seen. Skin as white as the snow, eyes like the night's sky, and hair that's even more silver than the coin. They're tall, slender people with long, pointed ears just like the Bleeding-Heart's people.

"Where are we?"

"We are in the Plum District. This area below us is the living quarters."

"Plum District, like the fruit?"

"Precisely." He nods. "They have the best, well, the *only* sugar plum jam in the entire Native. And they hold a festival every year during the last haul before Christmas. They invite all the other districts to join their festival and take a rest at their inns." He points to a small section of the district with a pop of color, and it seems like music blares from there. "Since the other districts work a little harder than the Plum District, they hold a festival to compensate for their easy work."

"What's their work?"

"Making wreathes. I'll show you." He pulls me away from the edge. I go slowly, still looking over and captivated by the beauty below. "They weren't always beautiful," Yonah says as he brings me to another view. We look off at the blanched land. It looks lackluster from here, just heaps of white snow, with people just as pale. They are beautiful, yet colorless. I suppose that God can even turn a monochrome land into a masterpiece.

"They were a small land of hardworking people who didn't have much. They were the poorest district, and eventually became overrun with mice and rats. By the time I arrived, everyone was working just to protect the little they had." The Guardian steps further onto the edge of the mountain. Below are the living quarters of the Plum District, but deep within the district where the only pop of color comes from, there's music playing and joy erupting in the streets.

"They didn't know there was a dark force at hand," Yonah says, returning my attention to their gloomy story. "Not so much of a force, but more of a *special* mouse." He looks over at me. "The Mouse King."

"The Mouse King? Like an actual mouse?"

Yonah laughs, his cheeks bunching. "Yes, if you can believe it. A demonic critter stood up on his hind legs and marched into battle with his smaller mice imps."

I can't help but laugh. I throw a hand up to wave Yonah

off as I say, "I don't mean to laugh at someone's troubles, but it is quite odd that a mouse was to blame for an entire district's fall."

Yonah agrees. "Then you'll be even more surprised when we run into the Fox of the North. He's the enemy of the nomadic wanderers up there. He and I are due for battle."

I gulp. "I don't think I can take another fight."

"At the very least, the Fox is the most normal looking. Krampus is half human and goat; the Mouse King is the size of a human; grey and as demonic looking as you can imagine. But the Fox of the North, just looks like a fox."

"But there's a catch, I bet."

"You're right. The Fox is a trickster of many kinds. He can manipulate time and space to make himself faster and stronger. While Krampus can cause illusions on contact, the dangerous aspect of the Fox is that he can cause illusions from a distance."

"So that means he can see you and suck you into a mirage?"

Yonah nods confidently, like none of this is threatening. "But he has to catch you when you're still. If you're moving, he can't entrap you."

I think for a moment, letting Yonah's words replay in my mind. "That's why those people are nomadic, isn't it? The people up north, they can't stop running, can they?"

"You are brilliant." Yonah smiles and reaches for my hand. I take his and we begin to walk down a snowy path. Yonah grabs the reins of the horses and pulls them along as we walk together.

"So, what spirit does the Mouse King represent in my world?"

"Good question," Yonah compliments. "The Mouse King represents death and disease in your world. Something you may have been affected by."

I bite my lip. "I'm not sure. But if it's here, then unfortunately, I probably have encountered it."

"Well, being here means you'll overcome it," Yonah says to cheer me up. I appreciate his enthusiasm, but I change the subject anyway to avoid worrying over who I've lost. There isn't really a point when you can't remember.

"Does battling these creatures scare you?"

"Not at all. I'm the Guardian of The Native, Belle. The only thing I fear is losing you." Of course, he says this with full confidence and a smile on his face.

I force myself to look away from his fiery gaze and into the freezing snow. I want to think chilly thoughts just to forget the warmth between our hands, but the silence feels awkward, so I ask, "How did you defeat the Mouse King?"

"He came to the Plum District in hopes of finding weak and feeble men standing ready with pitch forks and torches. But he found me, a single Guardian." He shrugs. "Long story short, I trapped the Mouse King. And the people have never forgotten that. It's why they send their holly wreathes around The Native for Christmas."

"I have a question about that, too." I stop walking, and Yonah does too. "Does everyone simply prepare for Christmas all year round?"

"We do. We prepare for The Native's celebration. Everyone travels to the central land of The Native for celebration from Christmas Eve through Christmas Day. And after Christmas, everyone helps clean up and returns home by the new year."

I gasp. "Really? *All year* just for Christmas?"

"It is a show of our faith that we trust that God is a promise keeper and will protect us another year; strengthen us, guide us." He pauses. "Jesus is the ultimate fulfilment of a promise. God prophesied that a savior would come back in the Garden of Eden, and everyone eagerly awaited Him." He tosses a hand up. "Of course, no one expected a baby, everyone wanted a man of war, like King David. And that's part of our celebration, too. Not only do we trust God to protect us and save us every year, but we trust that He has a plan no matter what form it comes in. A baby, a snowstorm, a small crop. You never know what God will do, but we trust that He will do something, and He always has."

My mouth twitches. I want to smile, but I know a part of me truly doesn't believe what Yonah said. It's hard when I know that something in the real world has kept me from believing in God. But being here helps me realize that even in a world as perfect as a dream world, evil still prowls. People still serve God despite their hardships. The Bleeding-Hearts serve God even when they owe the life of a child to a goat man, and He rescued them. This Plum District served God though a literal mouse terrorized them, and He rescued them and made them beautiful. And as far as I know, the nomadic people up north serve God, despite *still* being chased by an old trickster fox. They still believe in God, and He does have a plan to rescue them just like He's rescued everyone else.

I glance over at Yonah in the silence as we start walking again. He's a living, breathing, plan of God. Briefly, I truly try to think of who a walking plan of God in my waking life can be. It's to no avail, of course, since I can't remember anything.

"Everyone is someone I've met or will meet, right?"

"Yes and no."

I immediately stop. "Wait, that's not what you said initially."

"Initially, I could only tell you partial information."

My shoulders sag. "So, you're telling me that some of these people I won't or haven't met?"

"Some of the people you'll meet represent circumstances in your waking life. So, they may not be people you've met before, but they are certainly situations you've encountered and will likely encounter again."

I look out at the grey world that's beginning to gain its color. There's music and the smell of food fills the air the closer we get to the center of the district. I want to be angry, to flip out like Yonah had been lying all this time. But he's a Guardian, he can't lie, and he can only tell me the things God allows him to.

With a sigh, I ask, "Are there any more surprises or twists?"

"You'll just have to wait and see." Yonah gives me a small

smile. I roll my eyes and move to leave when he pulls on my hand. "Wait," he says as I turn back. "Look around you."

I glance around at the trees. They are blossoming, unlike the dead ones weighed down with snow we've been passing. "Are these holly trees?"

"They are. They are the specialty here."

"I thought you said the sugar plum jam was the specialty."

"Oh," he laughs, "that is the specialty they serve at the festival. But what they bring to the Christmas celebration is wreathes of holly."

I look back at the trees. They are tall trees with thin branches that could snap easily, which suggests the holly is light. The red berries sit beautifully on the shiny thick leaves. I wonder if I can eat the berries since this is the Plum District and it makes sense that the fruit would be edible. But Yonah's response shoots down my thoughts.

"The berries aren't edible in their raw form. You can only eat the cooked jam."

"Just the jam?"

"Well, you *could* eat the raw berries, but I wouldn't recommend doing that since they're poisonous."

I frown. "The berries are poisonous, the leaves are pointy, yet they bring them to celebrate the birth of Jesus?"

"Yes." He laughs. "But it's all symbolic of Christ." He points to the tree. "The spiky leaves are twisted into a wreathe to represent the crown of thorns Jesus endured. The poisonous yet beautiful berries represent that beauty can come out of something bad. The crucifixion was brutal and dark, killing our innocent Savior, the way the poisonous berry can kill us. But the beauty in the crucifixion is our freedom, and thus the red berry represents the blood that paid for us all."

"Oh…" The berries can only be eaten after they've been crushed and broken and cooked over a hot flame. Then they become a sweet, delectable treat for all to freely enjoy. It really is reminiscent of Christ; His perfect body being broken and destroyed for us to enjoy the sweet gift of salvation.

I reach for a leaf. "They are very beautiful."

"Would you like one?" Yonah grabs the bushy tree before I can reply. I watch as he gently tugs on a branch, cracking it, and breaking the single holly plant free. Sinking to one knee, and extending the plant, he says, "For my Belle."

I smile wide as I take the plant. "Thank you, Guardian."

"It is my pleasure."

I laugh and my heart swells with glee. "Get up, we still have to see the festival."

"Of course." Yonah stands and dusts the snow from his pants. "Come," he offers me his arm, "with the evening coming, the festival is about to begin."

I grab ahold of Yonah's arm and don't let go for the entire night. We walk through the booths, trying foods, and even playing games. Yonah is recognized so often that we don't get the chance to book a room at an inn. We end up stopping for a small chat at every booth. I'm tired of introducing myself by the time we reach the sugar plum jam booth.

The little booth is crowded with beautiful men cooking the fluffiest bread I've ever seen, and beautiful women are serving customers the jam and bread. Not to mention the long line Yonah and I are stuck in. But watching the men work hard to make the bread and anxiously counting the little jars of burgundy jam is exciting. The smell of candied fruit filled the air, on the wave of freshly baked bread. You can almost taste the bread in the air.

"I'm so excited," I say, squeezing Yonah's arm.

He pats my hand. "You've been so great this evening, introducing yourself over and over again. Sorry about that."

"Don't worry about it; this jam will make up for it, I think."

He tilts his head back, and his lush black hair falls over his shoulders as he laughs. "This jam will make up for it, I promise."

"And the bread?" I ask, admiring him.

"The bread will be the best—"

"Yonah!!" three voices chirp in unison.

The Guardian glances around, but it doesn't take long for him to find the three girls who called him. They are standing at the front of the booth, waiting for their order. Each girl has straight golden hair, eyes like the ocean, and faces like angels.

"Ladies." Yonah waves.

As the girls approach, he leans down and whispers, "These are the attendants to the leading fairy of this district. They are likely here to fill her sweet cravings. You were supposed to meet them tomorrow, but tonight will do."

I nod as the ladies come over. They're all smiles until they see me, and then they stiffen when they notice my hand clinging to the Guardian's arm. I shift to move away, but Yonah slaps his large hand over mine to keep it in place as he says, "Echo, Elektra, Eoghan." He nods at each one of the ladies as he says their names. "This is The Native's new Belle, Dontaye Jackson."

"Oh please," I try to sound modest, "Yonah always says that, but it's just a joke."

The women don't laugh, but Yonah makes it insufferable when he decides to tell them that I am *his* Belle.

"She's very sweet, isn't she? My Belle is too shy to be the Belle of the entire Native, so," he looks down at me with daring eyes and a charming smile before returning his gaze to the three ladies, "I'll keep her as my personal Belle."

"Well," Echo says, "you two seem very comfortable."

"We are very close," Yonah says matter-of-factly.

"I can see that." Echo's voice is tart. She tries to hide her completely unamused demeanor, but it's hard when her golden brows are flat, and she hasn't cracked a smile since she met me... none of them have.

"If I'm not mistaken," Elektra chimes in, she's taller than the other two and a little dopy, "Yonah, we were expecting you in the morning?"

"You are correct," he confirms. "You will see us in the morning. Tonight, I want to do something special for Belle. She's never had the sugar plum jam, and she's never been to one of these festivals, so we're spending the evening together."

"The evening?" Eoghan squeaks. Her worried eyes dart to the other three girls before Yonah confirms yet again. It's like he's *trying* to make everyone angry.

"Yes. I'm going to get her a room at an inn. Give her the full experience."

"Well, it may be difficult to find a room now since the festival has already begun," Echo says quickly—almost happily.

"For me?" Yonah smirks. "I am The Guardian of The Native. There is a room for me at every inn, in the hopes of me staying there."

Echo just nods, letting her eyes drop from Yonah to mine, just to burn holes into my face.

"Well, we better go," Elektra says, "we'll see you tomorrow." She turns to me. "Enjoy your bread and jam."

"Thank you," I say sorely.

The other two give me forced smiles as they follow Elektra. When they are out of sight, I snap to Yonah, but he's already smiling down at me.

"It'll be fine, I promise."

11

Dontaye

Yonah got me a private log cabin. There's a view from the window of the fireworks display that was the best in town. The log cabin people always saved that room for Yonah and were more than happy to rent it to him for the night. They offered it for the remainder of the festival, but Yonah refused it.

The cabin is spacious, having way more room than one person needs. There's a neat bathroom and three sofas crowded around the fireplace. Each has a different animal skin splayed across it; skins I assume come from my district. I also note that even though the floors are wooden, they don't squeak like the Dais's cabin floors. And there are two bedrooms, though my Guardian opted for a sleepless night outside my door. I heard him through the night having conversations with passersby. It was nice hearing Yonah interact with the others and their joy in seeing him. I find it overwhelming to have people love you from every district, but Yonah is immune to it. He's cordial and kind to everyone.

We set out early because Yonah wants to beat the morning festival rush. So, before the sun rises, we travel through the plum village to a large castle where soldiers stand guard. Each one is dressed in a shimmering blue jacket with intricate silver lapels. Shiny crystals decorate their shoulders as black belts cinch their waists. With silver pants and shimmery blue boots to match their jackets, these soldiers look whimsical with their bright pink cheeks and even brighter smiles. It's weird to see guards smiling the way they are, bearing their large teeth beneath their dark mustaches. They each look so similar, down to their whacky white hair that frizzes out from their tall hats, and their long beards.

"Who are these guys?" I ask as Yonah slows the cart.

"These are Nutcrackers."

"Really? Or are you just joking?"

"Nope. The Plum District was a poor district, and everyone worked hard before things changed. When I arrived, they wouldn't let me fight the Mouse King alone. Eventually, when their efforts were lost, they wanted my help, but they wouldn't stand by and let me defeat the Mouse King by myself. It was their problem and in their stubbornness, they found a way to help me."

I don't say anything, though that stubbornness and not wanting help sounds awfully familiar.

"A group of men gathered the only thing they had that every rodent loves."

"Nuts," I answer, though Yonah wasn't asking a question.

He nods anyway and continues. "That's right. Left a trail so long that it took two days to clean up. But once the district was restored, the leader of the Plum District deemed anyone who helped with the trail a Nutcracker. So, it became a position at the royal palace."

"Okay, but why are they all smiling?"

"It's a reminder of the cheer the district felt when they were finally freed from the Mouse King's grasp."

"Wow..." I watch the soldiers march in unison to cross paths in front of the castle. "So, these men are the ones who fought with you?"

"No." He laughs. "Well maybe one or two. Fairies tend to live a while."

I blink. "Did you just say *fairies*?"

"Yes, everyone here is a fairy. And the Sugar Plum Fairy is the leader of the Plum District. She's the only one who doesn't wear white, besides the Nutcrackers, of course."

"What color does she wear?"

"She wears purple." Yonah hops out of the cart. "Come, my Belle, it's time for you to meet fairies of the Plum District."

"If these people are fairies," I say as I take his hand and climb out the cart, "what were the people of the Bleeding-Heart District?"

"They are pixies, which is why Faire didn't believe in God, initially."

I tilt my head to look up at the Guardian as he offers me his arm. I hesitate since our closeness caused such a ruckus yesterday, but I also don't want to reject Yonah in front of the Nutcrackers, so I take his arm as I ask, "I don't understand why a pixie wouldn't believe in God. Actually, I don't understand how any of these creatures *can* believe in God. In my world, they're just imaginary fantasies."

He grins at me. "But this *is* a fantasy world, isn't it?"

I sigh.

"And even though it is a fantasy, it was still created by God. So, any living creature here has the capacity and the freedom to believe in Him and worship Him."

"So, why didn't the pixies?"

"Fairies are good natured from the start. But a pixie is like the bad alter ego of a fairy. Their initial nature is not of good character. They have to learn goodness, which is why they cling to God so much stronger than some of the other districts."

"Because they've learned to be good through God."

"Correct."

We make our way down the icy path leading to the front doors of the grand castle. It's grey and tall with peaks that pierce the clouds. There are windows that decorate nearly every inch of the castle. It's odd because even with all the windows, you still can't see inside.

As we approach the Nutcrackers, Yonah nods and one of the Nutcrackers turns to knock on the door. It gives a hollow sound that seems to echo through the entire district. The doors crack open, a whining noise bellows out and the snow around us swirls as the warm fragrant air from within gushes out at us. The three women from yesterday seem to appear out of thin air at the door. They are in long white gowns that reach the floor, their silky straight blonde hair rests on their shoulders, and their crystal grey eyes focus only on me.

"Good morning, Guardian and," Echo pauses to give me a once over, "Dontaye."

"Good morning, ladies, is the Sugar Plum here?"

"No," Echo says, dragging her eyes back to Yonah. "Though I am certain her arrival will shift things in the direction they ought to go in."

I glance up at Yonah who has a brow raised. "What direction is that, Echo? As far as I'm concerned, I'm the Guardian of The Native, which means I know which direction is best for all matters beneath the sun of our land." His bright eyes narrow and Yonah is the most rigid I've ever seen him as he says. "It would do you well to remember that."

"She meant no disrespect," Eoghan squeaks nervously.

Yonah raises a hand. "I'd like to hear that from her."

Echo clears her throat. "My apologies, Guardian Yonah, I meant no disrespect."

He nods. "Very well."

We stand in a tense silence, my eyes drifting to the bare white feet of the women against the silver floors.

"Well," Elektra's voice blurts into the silence. "The Sugar Plum will arrive soon, likely by lunch or sooner. She has to make an appearance at the festival this morning, so she should be returning soon. Until then, we can get you into your rooms and show you the house."

"Take Belle," Yonah says. "Show her around the castle.

I'll take her bags to the room." I glance up at my Guardian, pleading with the biggest eyes I can give him before he leans down and pecks my forehead. "They will take good care of you, don't worry."

I give him a nod before the three white fairies call in unison, "Please follow us." They turn and begin down the corridor, leading us from the main entrance where Yonah stands. I look back once more, worried that his kind words or stern warning wouldn't be enough to keep these three from heckling me while he's gone. My Guardian stands there, a hand on his hip, as he shifts his weight from one foot to the other. He raises a hand and waves, sending a bout of dizzying nostalgia over me.

Where has this happened before? A bad feeling paired with a goodbye? My thoughts torment me as I turn away to follow the ladies. They are leading me through the white, silver, and blue castle, but I'm not listening. They point at statues, ice sculptures, and other frozen pieces of art that decorate the castle. The stone walls are painted an icy blue, and the white marbled floor is lined with silver within the purposely cracked floor—that's the only thing I hear Echo say. Everything else is slipping in one ear and out the other. I'm consumed by the nostalgia, wondering where it came from and why it was so heavy.

It's almost like I can see the person who waved goodbye. The face of a man, yet I can't remember what he looks like. If I peel my eyes back enough, I'll be able to see through the blurriness. But no matter how hard I try, the light in my

131

memories only seems to dim.

Was he someone I was close to? Yonah told me that the people closest to us are the hardest to remember because we casually spend every day with them. But someone you don't see often has a stronger grip on your memories because you *want* to remember them in case you don't see them again. When a person is right by your side, you don't have to remember too deeply because they're right there to make another memory. However, those who are far, we cling to their memories because creating new ones may take a while or possibly, the chance to make a new memory may never come.

I stop walking and grab my head. Reaching for a wall to hold me up, I feel my chest tightening as the floor begins to blur.

"Dontaye? Are you alright?" The voice is indistinguishable. Everything is blurring, everything is beginning to look the same, all the white lights and frozen figures begin to fade as darkness overcomes me.

"Taye," Ezra said beside me.

"Hmm?"

"I … never mind."

I sat up on my elbow and looked over at him. With his hands behind his head, Ezra gazed up at the stars above. The night had fallen, and autumn's breeze washed over us as we watched the stars. It was something we started doing after we'd spent nearly a year apart. It was easier to talk beneath the stars, to focus on something else as you poured out your heart, your confusion, your loneliness. We told each other everything that really went on while we were separated. It was like that year apart had put a strain on us. It exasperated us. Sort of felt like we were just waiting to find each other again.

"You can tell me, Ezra," I said.

He shook his head. "Nah. I can't."

"Now I'm way too interested." I leaned over and shoved his shoulder. He laughed as he shifted in the grass. "Come on," I pestered, "tell me the truth. What's bothering you?"

His chest filled with air, expanding widely. I watched as he pushed the deep sigh from his lungs. His amber eyes lazily turned to me, but in that moment, no matter how lazy he pretended to be, something stirred within his eyes … something was always stirring within them.

"I don't know how to say this…" He adjusted, sitting up on one elbow, and smirked. "But I think you're the biggest loser on the planet."

I cackled and pushed him over. "I hate you, but …" I paused until his laughter calmed, then I turned over and moved to kneel beside him. I placed my hands on his chest and his eyes lingered on my hands before reaching my eyes. Glancing away, I whispered pathetically, "I hate you the most when you can't tell me the truth. When your heart is heavy."

I flow into consciousness, awakening to the sound of chatter. I sit up, shoving the heavy blankets back. This is the only place so far that doesn't have a fire inside the bedroom. It's just warm... weird. Scooting to the edge of the bed, I stare down at my feet against the pristine white floor. The tiles aren't cold at all, they are actually warm to the touch. I feel myself smiling as I look around the room. This fancy castle can only belong to a fancy person... a person I passed out before meeting.

I slap a hand to my face and sigh loudly. It's already embarrassing to be holding on to Yonah's arm in a place where I'm clearly not welcomed, and then to pass out the moment he's not holding me up... The embarrassment is unending in this fairy kingdom. I fall back on the bed and blink up at the ceiling.

"God, I don't know what I'm supposed to do here. I don't know what I'm supposed to learn from suppressed memories and dizzy spells. But," I swallow thickly, "I'm willing to try."

In the lingering silence, the chatter is still going on outside my door, but there are distinct voices close by. Close enough to almost make out the words being shared. I don't want to pry, but I do want to find Yonah for dinner and to give the Sugar Plum Fairy an apology for missing her return.

I roll out of bed and tiptoe to the door. I figure Yonah's right outside, since he was the night before. I crack the door to peek out, afraid one of those other fairies might see me if Yonah's not at my door. To my surprise, there's a beautiful, winged creature standing there with Yonah in the moonlight. His gaze narrows on her, focusing as she speaks softly. I assume this is supposed to be a private conversation, but the walls of this place are hollow and make even whispers easy to pick up. I watch as the winged woman talks. Her voice is laced with concern. The echoes of her worry reach me as I push open the door a little wider to hear better.

The Sugar Plum is a small woman with glossy purple skin and bright pink hair. She's the only pop of color in this entire district. Her short purple legs have green laces tied up them and a bright pink dress to match her afro hair puffing around her until it's just shy of her knees. I can hardly see her face, but I can only imagine the beauty she holds. I watch as she flaps wide wings. They are transparent, as if you're looking through a glass, possibly seeing the world the way a fairy would. The crystals that line the curves of her wings make them look like they've been dusted in sugar, as each crystal reflects in the moonlight. Worried purple hands go up in despair and briefly I wonder why she's purple. But Yonah's voice calls my attention back to their private conversation. "Clora," he says firmly, "she is the assignment."

Clora, or the Sugar Plum, shakes her head. "What about *me*, Yonah? What am I supposed to do?"

Yonah's eyes become weary as he glances down at the floor and then back at her. "I'm sorry, Clora. I'm her Guardian—"

Are they talking about me? I'm an assignment? Where have I heard that before...?

"So, I do not get to experience love? You get to fall in love, but I don't?"

135

My ears begin to burn as I try to make sense of the words the Sugar Plum Fairy spoke... *Who could Yonah be in love with?*

"We knew this was coming. What am I supposed to do? She's the—"

"*Assignment?* That's your only excuse," Clora says darkly. "All you want to tell me is that you've chosen her. If she wasn't the assignment, just some girl, what would your excuse be then, Yonah?" Clora snaps. "She's an *assignment.*" The word suddenly becomes a curse on her tongue that she hurls at Yonah as she goes on. "But falling in love wasn't part of the plan! You're her Guardian, not her *lover*! *I'm* the one you're supposed to love!"

Yonah's bright eyes study her for a moment. The moonlight seems to hug him, making him glisten beneath the white light. I cling to the door, squeezing the handle as my chest begins to tighten a little. Somehow, I've come between them, and I didn't even know.

Now, Yonah is *in love* with me? I instinctively place a hand to my chest as I watch him. He sighs and steps back, but Clora reaches out and grabs his sweater. "Please," her voice becomes even harder to hear. "You can't do this to me. Yonah, this was my last chance to—" I lean forward a little too much, and the door squeaks. Yonah's eyes immediately snap to mine, but it's the breathtaking beauty of the Sugar Plum that makes me gasp. Wide eyes the color of the ocean, and thick dark lashes. Her gentle cheekbones make her look womanly, though she's clearly no human woman. She looks like a butterfly that became a human.

Sucking in, I grapple for the door and snatch it shut.

"Dontaye," Yonah's voice comes behind the door in an instant, "let me explain what you overheard."

I sit on my bed and pull my knees into my chest. I'm just an assignment who's ruined everything. I don't need him to explain that to me. I don't *want* him to explain his feelings for me—if they were real or forced—because I'm just an assignment.

"Just go away," I say.

"Dontaye, please... I was going to tell you, but you needed time—"

"Was it me who needed time, or you, Yonah?" I shake my head. "Goodnight."

12

Dontaye

I wake up early the next morning and force myself not to think about the conversation between the Sugar Plum and Yonah. I'm just an assignment to him. None of this meant anything to him. Which makes sense because once I awaken, I'll disappear from this world. It's better just to be someone passing through than to make a mess and leave it behind.

I take my bag and load it on the back of the cart and wait in the darkness of the morning with the two horses. I doze off beneath a fleece blanket until I hear the snow crunch and feel the cart shake when he steps up.

"Good morning," the Guardian says.

I nod.

He chews his lip and glances around. "I see you were able to get your things loaded onto the cart."

"Yes."

"Good." He sits there for a moment before I feel him shift to look at me. I won't turn to see him; I just can't. "Well, we should get going then."

"Alright." I nod.

The ride is silent for a while, just the sound of the trotting horses with Yonah's occasional adjustment beside me. The bubble of silence we ride in is just beginning to get comfortable when I hear the Guardian clear his throat beside me.

"Listen," Yonah begins, but I cut him off.

"We don't have to talk about last night."

"I think we should."

"Well, I don't want to talk about anything complex."

"It's not complex." He shrugs and the weight of his wings sounds exhausting. "I want to explain to you what I meant when I called you an assignment."

"I'm just someone you have to help. I get it. That's your job. No explanation needed," I say bitterly. It wasn't easy listening to Yonah and Sugar Plum last night but hearing him call me an assignment after all the time we've spent together shattered my heart. I can't afford to live through some pathetic excuse, my shattered heart can't take anymore.

"Ms. Jackson…" Yonah slows the horses to a stop as the sun reaches through the trees to wash over us. "The assignment is the one we've been waiting for. When our world was created, it was created with purpose, as God is a very purposeful being. He is always planning." He chuckles as his eyes flee to the morning sun peeking between the trees. The light stretching across his face makes him glow, and he's as

139

captivating as the first day we met. "Everything that happened in this world, happened parallel to your world. And with time working so differently here, we have generations of people grow up here, waiting for the assignment."

"I don't understand what that means."

The Guardian gazes a little while longer at the sun, his square jaw and long neck radiant in the light. His strong shoulders hold up the weight of his wings and the entire world of The Native. He looks perfect sitting in his normal dark gear, and when his eyes meet mine, I feel my heart thump recklessly in my chest. In anticipation, in confusion, in desire. My heart is blurred with many reasons to thump wildly, but no matter how I try to fight it, there's one simple reason I can't admit to.

"The assignment is the one whose purpose will be fulfilled in this world. And once their purpose is fulfilled, our world will cease to exist."

"What?" I lean closer. "*What?*"

"When I told Sugar Plum you were the assignment, I wasn't telling her that to belittle you. I told her to prepare her for our last Christmas."

I swallow. "Why does this sound like your world is about to end because I'm here?"

"Because everyone and everything serves a purpose. We were created to serve a purpose in your life."

"No…" I shake my head. "No! This can't be!" I fumble with the fleece sitting over my legs to stand in the cart. "Yonah, please. Tell me that isn't the truth."

He looks away, and my heart sinks.

140

"How could God be so cruel?" I whisper.

"You're wrong," Yonah says gently. "It's like I said, we're people you know, people you'll meet, situations you'll encounter, or just lessons to be learned here. Which means you'll likely meet everyone again when you awaken."

"Except for the Dais family, and people who were created to teach me something." I choke on a sob and clutch my chest. "I can never come back here, can I?"

"Once you awaken, this world will cease, and you'll never be able to return."

I can't raise my head to see him. I don't want to look at him and know that I'll never see him again. I'll be stuck remembering people who I can never go back to. This world will end when I wake up.

"So, I won't wake up," I conclude. This seems good, and I can feel myself nodding. "Yes, I'll stay asleep! I'll never wake up!"

"You have to." Yonah laughs. "If you don't wake up, you'll die. And you won't be left here. Our world will still cease to exist no matter what."

"How can you laugh at this? How can you go around doing all of this?" I flare my hands out and say loudly, "How can you pretend to be happy? Why won't you blame me!?"

"Because," the Guardian reaches out and places a hand on my cheek, "I'm looking forward to seeing you when you wake up. In my true form."

"But you won't even remember this."

Yonah adjusts in the cart to hold my face with both his

hands. "So, remember for me, Belle. Remember so that you'll find me and make new memories with me. Ones that won't be temporary or connected to a timer. Remember me and find me."

I hiccup as I rest my hand on his forearm. "I will, Yonah. I will find you, and … and we'll…" I can't say it, but Yonah nods, giving me his warmest smile as he leans forward.

"Yes, we will."

The words we can't say, the things we really mean but aren't sure how to express, it all comes together when his lips press to mine. My heart is heavy, yet this warmth brings serenity to me, and my lips move without my permission. I kiss the Guardian back as the snow begins to fall around us.

When he pulls away, he still holds my face and says, "Sorry, I should've asked first."

I shake my head, feeling my ears burn. "No, that was perfect."

"May I kiss you once more, then?"

I nod shyly.

Yonah leans forward and kisses me once more, stealing every negative feeling and replacing it with a good one. A perfect one.

— ❦ —

We finally get moving again, traveling through the snowy world to go to our final destination. I'm not sure what to think or how to feel anymore, but Yonah gives me a reason to feel happy. He shed light on a horrifying situation and somehow still found it in him not to call God cruel.

I ponder this as our hands stay knitted during the ride. In a time where his life would end, his entire being would cease to exist, the world he knows and protects will simply stop, yet Yonah still loves and serves God. I always thought if I knew I was going to die I'd live wildly, not honorably the way Yonah and all of The Native has. However, in the face of death, Yonah still smiles. In my face… he still smiles.

"Dontaye," Yonah calls as he pulls on the reins of the horses. He leans out, pointing a gloved finger to something in the snow.

"What is it?" I lean over to look. It's a little hand poking from beneath the snow. I feel like freaking out, but Yonah reaches over the cart and pulls on the little hand, tugging it free from the snow.

I gasp loudly as he turns to me with a smile. "It's a doll, that means we're close."

Shoving a hand to my chest, I say, "Why does a *doll* mean we're close?"

"Because the Ginger Folk don't have a district, per say, they're nomadic. So, they traverse these woods and mountain areas all year long."

"Why don't they just settle down?" I ask as he passes me the little doll. It's brown, wearing a red dress with sparkly buttons down the front. Settling into my seat, I examine the doll while the Guardian gets the horses moving again, following the direction the doll was facing as he explains,

"Because they can't." His words are somber and filled with emotion. "These are the people tormented by the spirit of these woods."

Every hair on my neck shoots up, and it feels like the bitter cold whisking around us is suddenly icing my veins. Immediately, tormenting thoughts of Krampus comes back, and even though he's gone, he's the only spirit I know that's terrorizing this place.

"What... what kind of spirit is it?"

"A fox spirit."

I raise a brow, remembering Yonah mentioning a fox spirit he's supposed to face. It's almost unbelievable that a cute furry animal is chasing around these nomadic people.

"The Ginger District is full of people from every single district. They were traveling or making deliveries and passed through these woods. Or they went too far up the mountain and became trapped."

"Trapped in what?"

"In a nightmare." Yonah glances over at me. "The fox is a mischievous shapeshifting spirit who can cause illusions or nightmares. He can move faster than sound, which is why he's able to ensnare the travelers."

I nod. "Because he can hear them before they even know he's there."

"Exactly. And the next moment, he's appeared, pulling them into an illusion to eat them while they dream."

I inhale deeply and feel my mouth go dry. "How do you beat something like that? A shapeshifter, something that can move at the speed of sound? That means you have to be absolutely silent to win this fight."

Yonah shrugs casually as he looks ahead, completely unfazed by the fox spirit lurking about. He inhales deeply and releases the reins of the horses. "You only have to stay quiet if you don't know how to beat sound." He flexes his fingers and shakes out his hands. Without notice, my heart ticks up and my breathing increases. Something is already wrong.

Yonah looks over at me and smiles. "It'll be all right, Belle, don't worry. Take over the reins for me and keep going. Don't stop for any reason."

"Yonah—"

He slips a finger to his lips, instantly silencing me. His next words nearly stop my heart.

"He's already here."

13

The Guardian

With one push, I lift from the cart, setting my wings free to tear through the air. The moment I saw the doll, I knew we'd been lured into an illusion. When I initially spotted the hand sticking up through the snow, it was the hand of a child, small and bloody. The closer we got, the more blood appeared, and bodies began to appear as they lined the forest. The carriage even started to sink, as if the amount of blood on the snow had caused it to melt. It wasn't until I looked over at Dontaye, who seemed totally unfazed, that I realized I was in an illusion. And the moment I touched the doll's hand, the illusion dissipated, and I could see the fox's trail as he retreated.

Dontaye had been silent in the cart. She was just sitting there, but I wasn't. I was holding the reins of the horses, adjusting every so often. Even the shift in my cloak can ring for a thousand miles into the ears of a fox spirit. With their incredible hearing, not even the slightest sound could get by them. But that's because fox spirits are blind, so they rely on their excellent hearing to track their victims; from sound, they know how many are present and how far away are they.

For most people, defeating the fox spirit would be impossible. Even if he couldn't get you trapped in a nightmare, he was faster than sound and mischievous to boot. There was no telling what he'd do to paralyze his victims and eat them alive. However, as The Guardian of The Native, the fox spirit poses no undefeatable threat to me.

Pumping my wings, I rise higher into the air, glancing back to make sure Dontaye is still moving. She's frightened, but she's moving, bouncing with the rough trucking of the horses as they pick up their speed from a trot to a run. With their heavy hooves beating the snow, they will make enough noise to lure the fox out if he hasn't already pulled Dontaye into this illusion, too. I can at least rest easy knowing the horses, like all animals, will be unaffected by the illusion. Mercifully, they'll continue the journey to find the Ginger Folk and eventually snap Dontaye out of the fox's mind control by pulling her beyond his proximity.

I focus my vision on the sky above me as I fly beyond the clouds. They drench my wings, making me heavier and forcing me to work harder to fly, but I'm determined to find the light. To go beyond the blue and into the night. As the temperature begins to change and the pressure makes me lightheaded, I close my eyes and whisper a prayer.

"Jesus, You are the light of the world. Lend me Your

light."

Lightning whips through the sky and with a deep breath, I reach out and snatch it as it zips by. The crackling of the lightning in my hand rings out across the sky. Looking the bolt over, I smile, because the only thing faster than sound is light.

I ring the lightning bolt like a whip around me, covering myself with the light of Christ. Giving one strong thrust, I propel myself to earth, tucking my wings as I fly for a fast approach. As the clouds part for me, each one I pass is filled with lightning and follows me on my way down, twisting to make an electrified cyclone. As The Native becomes clear before me, I find the fox speeding towards the cart. On instinct, I flare my wings open for a rigid stop midair, then I suck in and heave forward, thrusting light from around me into the earth. It twists and dances on its way down with a screeching cry that disorients the fox.

It stops immediately, tripping on its four legs. Stumbling back, the fox begins to shake his head as the cluster of noise overloads his ears. With a clap, the sound of rolling thunder echoes across the sky and I shout as I lunge myself toward the fox. The cyclone follows me and threads the sky with twinkling white fog. The faster I move, the faster the fog races after me, until it catches me and wraps around me like a hand as I slam into the earth. The moment I touch the ground, a wave of light rolls through The Native, and clouds lift from the hovering fog to create cyclones to chase the light, destroying everything in its path.

Rising, I whip my lightning bolt at the fox. He dodges it

and rolls onto the ground. But he has to keep moving because a cyclone is right on his tail. Scampering away, the fox dodges the cyclone and rushes for a cave up ahead. I toss the lightning to the ground and lunge forward to step on it. I allow it to shoot me forward at its great speed, moving fast enough to start a current around me. As I pass the fox to reach the cave before him, I grab onto the stirring current of light and slam it into the ground of the cave. The entire stone floor cracks, and light bursts through the cracks.

When the fox arrives, he opens his mouth wide enough to break his jaw. Letting the lower half of his mouth sit slack on the floor of the cave, a dark mist begins to roll out, trying to cover the floor in darkness. Wielding the light like a sword, I run forward to the eyeless creature. With red fur, and black feet the size of a lion, the nine tailed fox lunges at me. With his mouth open, he heaves out a piercing noise that knocks me off my feet.

I'm hurled to the back of the cave, and before I can even register what's happened, the fox appears over me, trying to sink his teeth into me. The light I'm encased in shoots ahead and hangs itself around the fox's neck. The fox jerks back, wringing his neck and trying to fight his way free.

He shoves himself backwards, dragging the light with him. I shoot to my feet and stretch out a hand toward the fox, shouting, "Let there be light!"

The roar of the wind draws close as the lightning cyclones rush toward the mouth of the cave. The light hanging around the neck of the fox releases him but only for a split second. It begins to sizzle and morph until the sky crackles and the light shimmers so brightly I fall to the ground. Shielding my eyes, I look away as the light hollows out the ground to form an enclosure around the fox.

When the wind calms, and the shrieking of the fox is finally silenced, I lower my hand to see the fox frozen in a transparent cage. His ears are back, and each one of his nine tails is tucked in defeat as his mouth yawns open with a silent cry.

He will remain that way until judgement day.

14

Dontaye

The horses continue running and I lay low in the cart. The cracking of lightning, the sound of thunder and of shrieks all make me want to scream, but I hold it in until the noise of Yonah's battle with the fox is silent behind me. The moment I notice the silence, my heart begins to thump rapidly, and my eyes fill with tears. I sit up from the cart and pull on the reins to stop so I can scream. I don't even know why I want to scream; I know Yonah is fine, but the fear is still here. The nerves still rattle me.

"How did you know Yonah would be alright?"

I freeze in the cart at the voice. I lean forward and see the horses pressing their noses into the snow which means they haven't heard anything. I press my hand to my forehead as I sit back in the cart. "I'm tired," I say to myself, "it's all in my head."

"You may be tired, but you aren't hearing things, Dontaye."

I whirl around, looking for that same Voice. My eyes land on a man standing in the middle of the snowy clearing. He's wearing a long military style jacket that rests on the snow, leaving a trail of blue and silver cloth to follow Him. Heavy black boots with golden buckles have white pants tucked into them. Chestnut brown waves are sitting on His shoulders, and He's neither handsome nor beautiful... He's regal.

"Who... who are You?"

"It's not easy to recognize someone you don't know," He responds smoothly. "How could you recognize Me if you cannot recognize those who are represented here in The Native?"

I gulp and look around, wondering if Yonah would be here soon. "I-I can't remember them because I just can't."

"Is that the truth?"

I want to say yes, but something about this Man tells me that lying to Him would be devastating, or maybe it's His calm yet warm demeanor. His words are firm yet gentle, almost like every word is a guiding step, not just a sentence. He oozes with something that makes my heart stir. It isn't lust, that would pervert the purity in Him. It isn't kindness, though He *is* kind. It's something stronger, something you feel but, in His case, it's palpable. He's a walking talking figure of love.

"I've been told things, but I don't really know the Truth," I confess.

"You have spoken well. You do not know Me."

"You?" I whisper. "Who are you?"

"I am the Truth you are seeking. The Truth you've run from for so long."

I sit there, blinking at Him as He crosses the thick snow like it is flattened grass. He stands before my cart and raises a hand. I gasp when I see the hole in it; fresh, like He should've left a trail of blood in the snow.

"I'm going to show you something," He says.

Before I can protest, His fingers touch my forehead, and I feel myself fall slack.

When I open my eyes, a bright light burns them. I squint to take in the light before I sit up. The first thing I see are my legs... but I can see *through* them. My legs are transparent and so are my hands when I lift them.

"Don?"

I look over at the sound of my name, and gasp. Right in front of me, I can see my mother. She is standing at a door... my father's door. I turn to watch as my mother hesitates at the wooden barrier. She keeps one arm awkwardly stiff at her side as she raises the other hand.

"Don," she says again, "I'm sorry. I know I made you angry, but..." She swallows and says in a shaky voice, "I can be better. I promise." With hesitancy, my mother places a chestnut brown hand on the golden handle and turns it. "Don, don't shut me out," she says as she pushes open the door.

My father is sitting on the bed with a beer in his hand. He looks up at her with all the hatred in the world. "Get in here and shut the door," he says as he sets his beer down.

My mother steps inside and closes the door. She looks nervous as she stands in front of my father. The only light in the room comes from the candles on the bedside table and the dresser. The warm hues cast light on my father but shadows over my mother. When my father looks up, his piercing eyes take one look at her before he hurls a string of swear words at her.

"If you ever try to run away again, I'll kill you," he says, once the swearing is over.

Mother raises the hand she'd kept at her side. The light leaps off the steel of the weapon cradled in her palm. She racks the slide of the gun and shoves it at my father.

He throws his hands up immediately and snaps, "What do you think you're doing, Taylor!"

Her words come shakily, "Donald ... I'm taking Dontaye and we're leaving. But you're not coming with us."

My father jerks forward but my mother takes another step in her baggy pants and sweatshirt. "Do as I say, and no one gets hurt," she says.

My father lets out a chuckle before his body loses all the tension he'd been holding in before. "Taylor, you couldn't kill me if you tried."

"You're right," she says. "But don't test me. Turn over on the bed. Now."

"I'm not—"

"NOW!" my mother shouts.

With a smile on his face, my father concedes. He gives her a nod, like all of this is a joke, and turns over on the queen-sized bed. My mother moves as soon as he turns over. She grabs a pillow from the bed and shoves it over his head.

"What are you doing!?" He tries to shout and tries to throw her off of him. But my mother is determined. And desperate—dangerously so. She struggles to keep the pillow on his face as he attempts to turn over. Quickly, she lifts the gun and fires into the white pillow and my father stops struggling.

My mother pants as she stands over him, and his crimson blood begins to soak through the pillow, turning the lily-white threads to deep rouge. She moves fast to the bathroom and grabs a wet wipe to clean the gun and then wraps it in the cloth and carries it to my father's body.

When she snatches the pillow away, she jerks back at his blood and the sight of his head, burst open and singed around the bullet hole. Her hands begin to shake, and she takes a step back, like reality just hit her, but something else calls to her... *someone* else.

"Mommy?" I hear my own voice. It's the voice from my childhood, wandering the halls to find my mother. At my call, she snaps back and grabs my father's hand from the bed and puts the gun in it. She races around the room, grabbing every other candle to sit them on the floor. She sets one by the window where the long drapes hang low enough to catch, then she places the bloody pillow there, too, and tips the candle over. It catches fire to the drapes and then the pillow before

155

my mother runs out of the room and down the hall to find me. When she does, she tells me to be quiet and act normally.

My eyes fill with tears as I watch.

I remember this day... The words are a whisper in the back of my mind. My mother took a single duffle bag, and I had a backpack that she'd prepacked for me, and we left the apartment building. We took the stairs because there were no cameras there, and we took the back alleys for the same reason. I didn't know what had actually happened until much later. All I knew was that my mother was taking me on an adventure to grandma's house.

The low conversations they had were filled with tension. My grandmother didn't like what'd happened, but she loved my mother and let us stay with her for a while. She even covered for my mother when the cops came. She told them my mother and I showed up a while back for the weekend—like we always did. The cops brought my mother's performance and my grandmother's, too. In fact, the investigators didn't find any foul play. My father's death was ruled a suicide by the small amount of evidence left behind. The apartment had been scorched in the fire, and a few others were too, so there wasn't much evidence to recover. Thankfully, the only person who died that night was my father. My mother got away with killing him and when I found out the truth, I began to hate her.

"Why am I reliving this?" I say aloud as I watch my mother through my memories.

"Because there are things that you don't know," the Voice says.

I glance around but no one is there. A wind blows and the scene before me begins to rewind. It goes back to the time before my mother killed my father. Snippets of my mother being beaten. Snippets of my father cheating on my mother. Snippets of my father sexually abusing my mother. Snippets of my mother weeping as she tried to cover her scars and bruises. And snippets of my mother smiling when she sees me. Hugging me a little tighter when I wrapped my arms around her.

Time fast forwards again, and I can see my mother close to her death day. She had many boyfriends after my father, but none of them stayed around. They always left her. A vision plays of my mother sitting in an empty bedroom alone. Another vision shows her standing outside my door with her hands covering her face, her body trembling. We'd argued and I told her I hated her for killing dad. A replay of my mother at my grandmother's funeral, weeping as the only person in the world who still cared for her was lowered into the ground. Time after time, I watch the replays of my mother weeping, crying, begging God to free her from this misery. Begging God to protect me. The night before she died in an accident, she cried out to God and told Him that she just wanted to be loved again. She wanted me to love her, but she knew I never would. So, she asked God to reach me, and to someday tell me the truth. Tell me that she'd done it all for me.

The moment her prayer left her lips, every snippet and vision I saw replayed again, but this time, *everything* was shown to me. My father was not the man I always believed he was. He was evil and wanted to hurt me, but my mother would give herself instead. The boyfriends she had, were men she slept with to make ends meet before she got saved. The men from the church who'd help her out financially would visit the house at night for repayment—until someone found out and shamed her. They only ostracized *her* from the church, not the men she'd entertained for money. Eventually, she got a job, but that wasn't always enough, and we went without. That was when my heart hardened towards God. When the church ostracized her and not the men. When God didn't intervene, but my mother still served Him. When we were broke, but my mother still gave her tithes to whatever church she could find, or she sent them online. Everything made me angry. And I blamed my mother for it all until I began blaming God instead.

— 🌿 —

I blink and He steps away, lowering His fingers from my forehead.

"You showed me that?"

"I did," He says.

"And You… You were there, weren't You?"

"I was."

"Who are You!?" I scream. "Why didn't You help her?"

"You know that I am the Truth."

My heart shatters open. "I hate You! I hate You!" I scream at the top of my lungs. I know exactly who He is. I'd pushed all thoughts of Him away because life was hard. I thought He should've saved me from all of this since I was innocent. He should've saved my mother when she turned to Him. I blamed Him for all of our shortcomings... I blamed the One who saves. I blamed Jesus.

"You are angry," He says gently, "but you don't have to be. I saved you at the request of your mother and My Father."

"But You knew we needed You a long time ago!" I scream. "Why wouldn't You just help us?"

"Because if I had helped back then, you wouldn't have developed true faith. You would have believed in Me because of nice, convenient miracles. But you wouldn't have truly gotten to know Me the way your mother did. The way your mother *wanted* you to know Me."

"So, You left me in bitter anger, resentful and confused my entire life? For *You?*" I shake my head as I wipe my nose. "This is about You. Everything is all about You with no regards to ANYONE ELSE!"

"No," He shakes His head, "this is about you."

"How?" I hiccup. "How can any of this be about me?"

"Because your mother was always destined to have a short life. She needed to come home before it was overwhelming for her. However," He pauses and gives me a smile, "you are much stronger than your mother, and are destined for much more."

I stare at Him, unable to form words as He goes on.

"If I had helped, you would've had a *form* of godliness, but heaven would be unattainable for you."

I back further into the cart, bumping into and shaking the whole thing, but Jesus doesn't stop explaining. "People think

God wants bad things to happen, but that isn't true. There are times when He will allow bad things to happen even to the most innocent of His children, because every trial is a testimony. Every trial where My brothers and sisters succeed is a testimony to onlookers and even to themselves. It is a testimony to all of Heaven. We bear witness to your trials, the Spirit bears witness and reminds you that you are an overcomer in Me." Jesus comes closer, but I don't want Him to. "In Heaven, the angels learn a little more about God through His creation every day. And when Satan comes to accuse you, the trials the heavens have witnessed are brought to his attention. He is reminded that you are an overcomer, and your strength comes from Me, so he cannot harm you."

"Yeah," I nod, "because God does all the harming."

"God does all the teaching. Lessons are hard to learn depending on the test and trial, but there is never a test that God gives you that you cannot pass."

"YES, THERE IS!" I yell. "How can hating my mother my entire life just to find out the truth *after* she's dead be a test? That's my life—my *entire* life has changed! This isn't a game!"

Compassion rolls over Him to reach me. My heart begins to hurt as I look Him in the eyes. Eyes that hold the world and can sweep me away if I wasn't so angry. So angry because I understand His words completely, I just don't want to accept them. I don't want to accept that this was for me, no matter how bad it seemed, no matter how painful my entire life has been; losing my mother, being confused and hurt was entirely for me. And with this truth, I have a chance at a second life.

A second chance to make things right, that's what I was supposed to do every time I learned something about my mother's past or about God. I was supposed to take that chance to give up my anger and see things differently, but I didn't. Instead, I used it as fuel for hatred. Hatred for her, hatred for God, hatred for myself for hating everything. I stayed in a cycle of existing but never really living. Anger held me back from the One who wanted to set me free. But I just couldn't turn to Him. I didn't want to learn the truth because I feared it. I feared that the only reason my mother would kill my father is because we were in danger. I feared that God always had a plan for me despite what it looked like. Because if any of that was true, then I'd spent my life angry and bitter for no reason. I'd have so many regrets, but the pride of my heart wouldn't let me feel any other way. I had to blame God, because if I didn't blame Him, then I could only blame myself.

It's very clear in the scripture that we are to die to ourselves and rise to a new life. Dying to our old selves means losing everything that connects you to the world and to your life of sin. That is why God told Abraham to get away from his kindred. That is why Jesus told the rich man to sell all of his possessions. We have to lose everything, and then be taken to a place of growth. A place where we develop into who we're supposed to be. Like John the Baptist was a voice in the wilderness, Samuel was left at the temple to grow in his calling, and King David was sent into the wilderness. When God calls us, *He* takes us through a time of learning and shedding the old skin. He leads us beside still waters, in the path of

161

righteousness, allowing His rod and staff to comfort us. The wilderness, the valley of the shadow of death, are supposed to be places of growth and discipline, not a dwelling place. And for me, I've dwelled there for so long that I don't want to come out.

It's easier to blame God than it is to just accept His will. It's easier to tell Him that He's not fair than to simply obey Him. It's easier to walk away instead of addressing your problems. Because turning on the light in a dark situation exposes everything. All matters of life, every problem, and every good thing is exposed, too. Not revealed... everything is *exposed.*

What do you do then? How do you keep going with everything under a light?

You either make the adjustment or you back away from the light.

I backed away, though I knew I shouldn't have. I knew my mom would've wanted me to pursue God, but I just couldn't. I threw up walls and barriers with proximity alarms so if I even thought too long about God, I would force myself to think about something else. To go find something evil to do. I'd do anything to fight the love of God that banged recklessly at my heart.

"But now," I whisper, "I can't ignore You like I want to. You're taking away the anger, the frustration, the guilt, and the pain." I bite my lip, trying to hold in the tears of hidden relief. "I wanted this freedom so badly, but I was so angry at You because I was really angry at myself."

Jesus comes closer and steps into the cart. He pulls me into His loving embrace and says, "I can bear the weight of your anger, and frustration. I have felt all things on the cross, and I know how you feel. My shoulders can carry your hurt, but yours cannot. So, give Me this pain, give Me your anger, and I will give you My peace and My joy. I will take away your guilt and give you redemption. I will restore you."

I nod against Him, sobbing loudly as I grip His jacket. "Please take it all away!"

"Be set free in Me, Dontaye."

15

Dontaye

I sit in the cart alone and stare down at my hands. I'm thankful I can remember Jesus being here and the experience He gave me. I try not to let the regret overwhelm me; knowing that I'd been angry at my mother and God wasn't just disappointing, it was embarrassing. It took me years to finally let go, and if I had long ago, I never would've come to The Native. My mother might've died loved.

I sink my face to my hands to cry when I hear the voice of a child, "Miss?"

I snap my head up to find a little child, cute as a button, with cocoa brown... fur. He looks like something crossed between a bear and a fairy with his rounded ears on top, and thick black whiskers on a beautiful face.

"Y-Y-Yes?" I respond.

The little boy cocks his head to the side. "Why are you

alone out here crying?"

"Funny," I wipe my tears, "why are you out here alone?"

"I'm not. My people are coming. I'm hiding from my sister." He flashes me a wide smile and slips a finger to his mouth that sports a sharp nail. He backs away with a wicked grin, and turns to run deeper into the forest, showing off his fluffy red tail. I gasp when, in the distance, he drops to all four and gallops faster than he was running on just two legs. I would've watched until he disappeared as a red splotch into the winter's grey, but the sound of shuffling catches my attention over my shoulder.

A cinnamon brown girl, identical to the bear-boy who just whisked away, comes up to the cart and asks, "Have you seen my brother?"

"I—"

"Red! Did you find…" the voice of a woman trails off as she approaches the cart. She blinks at me with cat-like eyes and perky fairy ears. She has striking red hair, like the people of the Bleeding-Heart District, but she has whiskers like the two children I just encountered. The only difference between her and the children is that they look like bears, and she looks like a mystical woman. Tall and strong with thick shoulders and course arms hidden beneath her animal pelt that shifts with every movement.

She slams her stick into the snow, it stays erect as she eases to the cart with caution. Hovering over me with her great height, she says in a cunningly smooth voice, "Who are you?"

"I-I…"

"Easy, Berry," the voice of my Guardian resounds through the wintery forest, and I've never been so relieved to hear him. He appears almost out of thin air when I glance around and find him standing beside the woman he just called Berry.

When our eyes meet, I crack.

"Yonah!" I cry as I shuffle from the cart. I gather my dress and trip down the step into his arms. I feel relieved as he holds me, stroking my hair and whispering that he's here, telling me that I'll be alright. I don't even care that Berry's standing there, I'm so overwhelmed that some sort of normalcy has returned with Yonah.

"Are you alright, Belle?"

I nod, sucking in a deep breath to calm myself. "Yes, I'm alright."

"I'm sorry it took me so long."

"It's okay."

Yonah steps back and tilts my chin up. His warm smile and bright eyes stun me with comfort. I didn't know that I'd been so dependent on him this whole time.

"Red," the little boy's voice fills the air, calling all of our attention to him. He's standing by the horses with his arms crossed over his chest and a tight frown. "You didn't come looking for me," he complains.

"Momma stopped me," Red sounds apologetic as she passes Yonah to meet her brother. She offers him a hug he doesn't want initially, but he gives in anyways.

"Dontaye," Yonah says, "I want you to meet the head

family of the Ginger Folk, Cranberry and her twins, Red and Crimson—Crim for short."

I nod at the three mystical humanoid creatures.

"I wasn't expecting to meet you so soon." Berry looks me over and her cat eyes flick to Yonah as she addresses him, "This is the one."

"You've always been so bright, Berry," he says.

She looks down at her two children who are caught up in their own antics, which involve fluffing the snow off of Crim's tail. "My babies will forever be children, I suppose."

There's silence among us. I stand there still clinging to Yonah as The Guardian and Berry offer a silent exchange. Berry's chin rises a little before she gives Yonah a nod.

"They are free to run now," Yonah says, breaking the silence.

"We can run?" the twins ask simultaneously. Their synchronized answer reminds me of the twins at home, Aconite and Winter. I hadn't thought of Rachel and the family back in the Forest District nearly this entire time, but now I wish to see them.

Yonah leans down, burying one knee in the snow as his heavy cloak covers the earth. He reaches for the twins and each one takes a hand. "That fox won't catch you now. You're free to run, run, run as fast as you can."

"He couldn't catch us anyways," Crimson says proudly, "because we're Ginger Folk."

"And us Ginger bred folk are the fastest out of all the districts," Red adds.

"Really? And why's that?" Yonah taunts playfully, but I know he's doing this so I can learn more about the nomadic people.

The little girl takes the bait. "Because our ancestors were cave dwellers who could run faster than horses. They got all their energy from eating and hibernating during the heaviest part of the winter, so when they woke up, they could sprint for miles to find new land."

"That's right." Yonah nods. "Crimson, what else makes you special?"

"Our ears." He grabs his round ears and blurts, "These came from our ancestors, but Mommy's ears came from the other people."

"What people?"

"The fairies and the bleeding people who came here but couldn't leave because of the fox."

Yonah smiles proudly. "So, your mother is a cross between the original cave people, a fairy, and someone from the Bleeding-Heart district?"

The twins nod and Red says happily, "And our father was from there, too!"

"What happened to him?" I ask, placing a hand on Yonah's shoulder. I want to seem friendly, and the children are very welcoming to me. I catch Berry's expression. Her dead eyes wash over me before turning to look over the trail they'd followed up here.

"Our father died," Red says sheepishly. "Mommy was in labor when the fox attacked."

My eyes leave the little girl to find Cranberry turned completely away to head down the path she'd come from. I can't find any words to say, so I stand there and watch as she disappears into the wintery mix.

"You two run along and catch up with your mother. We'll come to your camp a little later, okay?" Yonah instructs.

The two little red bears nod and run off, racing each other and filling the forest with their cheer. Yonah and I watch in silence as he slowly rises to his feet. He takes my hand as a fresh layer of snow begins to fall.

"Are you okay?"

I sigh. "So much happened today, I don't know if I'll ever be okay."

"So, He came to visit you."

I snap my head up to stare at him. He's still watching ahead as the falling snow fills the silence until I find my voice. "How'd you know?"

"Earlier, there was a barrier of light blocking me from finding you. He's the only One who can emit that much light."

"Jesus, He came and showed me something from my waking life."

Yonah takes a breath as he listens.

"He showed me the truth and I was finally able to accept it." The lump in the back of my throat feels like a rock as I stand there in the frozen cold with Yonah. I begin to tremble, and I don't know if it's because I'm cold or fighting tears again, for the hundredth time today.

"Do you know why we prepare for Christmas all year

long?" His question throws me off guard, but Yonah doesn't wait for a response. "It's because we're in constant anticipation of the promised birth of our Savior."

"But Jesus already came, right?"

"Indeed, but we don't see Christmas as a mere reminder of His birth in the past. The Native sees Christmas as a constant celebration of His birth and a *rebirth* of what comes with it." He smiles. "Christmas is a release of blessings."

I nod slowly.

"We spend all year exhibiting our faith in God, believing that this Christmas He'll defeat Krampus, or the Nine-Tailed Fox. That this year, someone will get married, they'll have children, the promise will come. Just like the promised Savior came." I turn to look up at Yonah as he says, "We knew He'll fulfill His promises, even if we never see them. So, we wait and look to the Heavens as Abraham did. He may not have seen his descendants numbered like the sand in his lifetime, but God kept His word. We know that even if we don't see His promises in this life, we'll see it in yours." Yonah looks down at me and pulls me close, draping his strong arm over my shoulders. "I'm so proud of you, Dontaye. You did good."

"Why does this feel like goodbye? I barely understand anything."

"It's not goodbye." He laughs, and I feel the tightness in my chest easing. "I just wanted you to understand why we celebrate Christmas."

I squint. "But why now, when I told you that Jesus visited me?"

"Because The Native has been waiting in anticipation not just for Jesus, but for you, too. We knew that once you arrived, we'd begin to enjoy the greatest time of our lives, yet the most sorrowful. We'd realize all the things we'd left undone while simultaneously having blessings and promises fulfilled and manifested."

I move from beneath his arm. "I don't... I..." I have no idea what to say. It's not like he hasn't told me before but hearing it all over again makes this all seem so villainous rather than heroic. However, there's a dull feeling in the back of my mind, reminding me that these people always knew the end would come at some point. It's a reminder that I don't have to feel responsible, even though I truly do.

"There is nothing I could do. I was always supposed to come here and end this dream."

The Guardian steps forward and raises a hand. The snow around us freezes in time and the world suddenly becomes still and soundless. Taking my hands in his, he says, "When I became a Guardian, God told me that He'd grant one special request for me since all the power He'd given me was for *His* glory. He told me I could ask for anything, and so I asked for this." He moves his gloved hand through the air, dodging the snowflakes. "I asked God to let me freeze time. He was moved with compassion and granted the request."

I cover my mouth and stare at the world around us. "Why now? Why stop time now? Why for me?"

"Because there's something about someone finding the Light that makes them even more beautiful than before. And I wanted to stay in this moment a little longer." He steps closer, closing the gap between us. He wraps his arms around my waist as I let him draw me into his chest. I stare at his firm frame hidden beneath his dark sweater and heavy cloak. Tracing up his frame, I interlace my fingers behind his neck. He's staring at me, and for the first time, I see a flicker of sadness in his eyes. All this time, The Guardian of The Native has been strong and unwavering about the demise of his world. However, today, I see the sadness there, the emotions he's been hiding.

"Yonah," I whisper. "I don't want this moment to end."

He smiles and presses his forehead to mine. "In a perfect world, I'd stay like this forever with you." As his lips press to mine, I feel my entire body fill with emotion. I could taste the bittersweet desire to stay and to continue this journey on his lips, but no matter how bitter the taste, I don't want it to end. Because with that bitterness comes the sweetness of life, one I've tasted before.

Before Yonah can pull away, the wind howls, and the snow begins to fall again.

Time has begun again, and we both know the end is near.

16

Dontaye

When time begins again it seems like it has sped up. Yonah and I decide to camp just outside the nomadic Ginger Folk campsite. He explained he didn't want me in their camp last night because they would be feasting until sunrise over the defeat of the fox. Which, initially, that's what we'd come here for, according to my Guardian. However, after learning that her children would never grow up, Berry was less than happy to have me at the party. Well, it may come as a surprise, but the feeling was mutual. I didn't really want to go to a feast for the death of their enemy knowing that their time was up. My own guilt was eating away at me, though it was no fault of my own. I still felt responsible and helpless.

None of that stops Yonah from driving our cart deeper into the forest where the Ginger campsite is this morning.

"They'll be easy to find now since the fox is gone," Yonah

says as he holds the reins.

"Were they hard to find before?"

"Very. They would hide in complete silence most days, only using sign language to communicate. There were times, like yesterday, when they were far enough away from a regular trail that they'd speak and run and make noise. But generally, those people are very quiet."

"They've spent their lives in silence, but now they're free and they're still bound. Time is not fair."

Yonah takes my hand in his. "Time is what you make of it. You can waste it or use what you have to make it worth something."

I choose not to say anything else as Yonah steers us to the Ginger Folk's campsite. I can smell it before I see it. The smell of cloves and cinnamon, something else warm and resonating, mingles in the air as the horses cart us closer.

"Do you smell that sweetness?" Yonah asks with a smile.

"I do, but I can't name it."

"Molasses."

I inhale deeply and my body shivers with warmth and excitement.

"This is an ancient recipe," Yonah explains. "The Ginger Folk stopped making this sweet treat a long time ago once the fox tracked them down. He followed the sweet smell until he found their camp."

"So, what did they cook with after that?"

"They stopped eating meat and sweets. They only ate vegetables they could gather in these snowy mountains. When they occasionally had meat, they would season it with dark and bitter herbs to scare away the fox spirit. He never bothered them when they made bitter herbs. It was strong enough to draw the fox, but potent enough to disrupt his senses."

I nod. "I see. So, they ate bitter food?"

"They did. But now they don't have to. They're free now." Yonah raises a hand and waves it through the air to show me the expanse of the Ginger Camp. For miles, there are tents set up, and people still dancing and celebrating.

"I guess the celebration is still going," I say to Yonah.

He laughs beside me and agrees with a head bob.

"Yonah," the voice belongs to Cranberry who approaches from behind our cart. I jump at her voice, but Yonah remains still, watching her come around the front with a smile. *I bet he knew she was there all along.*

"I knew we wouldn't need to go far to say goodbye. I just hoped we'd get to be a little closer," Yonah says to Cranberry.

Her eyes flee to mine and then back to Yonah's. "We are grateful for what you've done for us."

"Be grateful to God, not me," Yonah instructs.

Cranberry dips her head, and her vibrant hair and skin scream out against the white blanketed world. "I will send word to my people that you have continued on your journey, Guardian. But I will not tell them their fate, I do not wish to bear the weight of their sadness."

Yonah doesn't speak for a second. He just looks at Cranberry, and I am left wondering what he's thinking. His face is tense and his eyes narrow, but he doesn't look angry, just focused.

"Cranberry, the information you know is not yours to withhold. I entrust you with the knowledge of the end. You do not get to bask in the joys of your people without bearing the weight of their pain." Yonah lowers his eyes to the snow and says sharply. "You have but a district, the smallest in The Native, to bear the pain for." His eyes snap to hers. "I have the entire Native to bear upon my shoulders." There's a crisp and hollow moment of silence where I feel afraid to breathe. If my breath is just a hiss too loud, one of them will snap.

"My Guardian, you must remember that I am only—"

"No, *you* must remember," Yonah says loudly as he surges to his feet, "that my words come from Him. And my commands are His. You will do well to never forget it even when there is only a fraction of a second left of this world, and time has been eaten away from you." Yonah's thick cloak ripples out and scatters all around him. I can hear the movement of the heavy material, weighing down the wind as it is cast around the Guardian from his swift movement. Cranberry cowers away as Yonah stands and the horses cry too, stomping their hooves nervously. The sky rolls out a dark cloud that saps all the light from The Native and holds it in its bosom to strike through the sky as searing bolts of lightning.

The world reacts to his feelings... Yonah is more than just a Guardian, he's the heartbeat of this world. If he loses himself, the entire Native loses too.

Shakily, I reach up and touch Yonah's hand. His hand twitches and I see his jaw clench beneath his perfect skin. He takes a breath and says, "You will tell your people and see that they have more faith and love for God than you do." The Guardian flares his cloak out to sit and grabs the reins. "Goodbye, Cranberry."

Cranberry acknowledges him with a nod, but nothing else.

Our cart takes off, but I keep my hand in Yonah's. I don't look back because I don't want to see if Cranberry is crying or angry. I know I'm the cause for all of this but it's not like I chose this.

"Don't blame yourself," Yonah's voice is calm again. "Cranberry will get over herself. And even if she never does, that is for her to decide.

"Is it true the rest of the Ginger Folk will accept this?"

Yonah looks at me, and I'm almost frightened of him. The intensity in his eyes hasn't dulled, so he looks intimidating, and it feels like he's looking through me and not at me.

"It is true. I don't want you worrying about that, okay?"

I nod and stay silent. For the first time in a while, I want to wake up. Not to see the boy I can't remember or see the life I'm living in the waking. I want to wake up so that this misery can be over. Knowing that these people don't even get to die, they'll never get to reunite in heaven, they'll simply stop existing, is too much to bear.

Our journey home is mostly silent, and the only warmth we share is between our hands. We hold hands like separating might push us too far apart and remind us of our differences.

That I'm meant to end this world, while Yonah's meant to save it. I can't imagine how difficult this journey truly was for him. He had to face every district's leader and tell them the time had come for them to say their last goodbyes. He had to deal with the weight of that news and with me not understanding anything. And he did it all while smiling.

The thought makes me look over at him. He's watching ahead, still and focused. He doesn't look tense anymore, rather, the Guardian of The Native looks relaxed, relieved almost. His broad shoulders aren't tight, and his jaw isn't locked, there's no scowl and he's not gripping the reins. Yonah rides alongside me, content with himself. He finished his job and is now returning me home safely. I wonder what the Guardian's going to do until Christmas.

I look out at the snow as it falls in the pink sunlight now. It looks pretty, dropping from Heaven as fresh powder to blanket the entire realm of The Native. I lean my head back and stare up at the sky.

"Searching for something?" Yonah breaks our silence, and I say, "No, I just realize that somewhere beyond this pink sky is another version of me lying asleep. I wish so badly that she could be here to experience this. To never forget this." Tears prick the backs of my eyes. "Instead, she'll wake up and wonder why Christmas means so much."

"Isn't it easier to forget the ones you can never see again?" Yonah asks simply. It's such a plain statement that makes sense, yet I don't want to accept it. I don't like it.

"Yonah—"

"When you first arrived," he says, still looking out at the snow ahead of us. In the distance, smoke is billowing lightly, disrupting the falling snow. It offers a screen for the pink sunlight to pierce through. But the smoke doesn't bother either of us, the white air is an indicator that somewhere nearby there is warmth. An entire district of people are warm.

"You wanted to go home," Yonah continues, "you wanted to wake up as fast as possible. But slowly, this world began to mean so much to you that you were willing to stay and forget the real world. You didn't realize the dreams of your waking life were growing less and less by the day. And the desire for a life awake from The Native was nearly gone." Yonah turns to look at me, and his face remains constant, the way it always has. Warm, delightful, beautiful. The things anyone wants to see, except for me. I don't want to see Yonah's plastered smile and perfect teeth. I want to see his tears and the burning desire for me to stay written all over his face.

"So…" he says as he pulls the straps of the horses.

I glance out and see the district below. People mosey about, likely finishing Christmas decorations and whatnot.

"One day," Yonah catches my attention again and when I turn to him, he reaches up and brushes a lock of hair away from my face. "The Belle of The Native will grow old in her world. And she'll be filled with so much joy. She'll have lived a life full of laughter and joy, and love." Yonah pauses for a second and I hear it… his voice hitches, but he tries to restrain the emotions. "One day, she will look at a journal where she tried to write down what she remembered from this dream and wonder why something so trivial as a dream meant so much. One day," he says again, and my tears begin to fall. Yonah wipes one away. "My name won't be remembered. All that will be remembered is that you found Jesus when you needed Him most. He was there. That's what will remain."

"Yonah," my voice trembles as I whisper to him. "Please…" I don't know what I'm pleading for. There is nothing more that I nor Yonah can do. "Why… Why can't things be different? Why does it have to hurt?"

"God is fair and just, no matter how painful it feels. This is for your good."

"What about yours?" I ask. "What about *you*?"

My Guardian offers me a broken smile. "Some dishes are made to be thrown away. Others are made for décor, and all the more, some are made for use."

I begin to sob into his chest. Yonah wraps his arms around me, and I weep until I am heaving dry tears. I want more time; I want something to change. But sometimes things don't change, and you have to accept it.

After composing myself, Yonah drives me home. Through the narrow neck of the woods that spills into the marketplace of my district. I watch the people packing up for the night. They all stop to wave to Yonah, and the woman that the Dais's waved to when I first arrived is there again. In her big puffy jacket with the thick fur lining, she waves frantically at Yonah, and once again at me. This time, I raise a hand and nod. I try to offer a smile, but my emotions are still twisted with guilt and sadness, so my smile is only halfway present.

That only stirs the woman all the more. She looks so happy that I've waved back, she even begins to wave harder. I can feel myself chuckling inside as I wave a little more as we pass by.

The joy of The Native is contagious. These are people who are well aware of what my presence means. For some, like the Sugar Plum Fairy, it is painful. For others, it makes them angry like Cranberry. But, for some like Faire and Charlie and Rachel, they welcome what is coming. They love God enough to let their own existence go. People who won't ever see Heaven (nor Hell), still choose to believe in the God of Heaven. They choose to believe in Him and His principles and to follow them, despite no promise of a better life after death. These are the people I wish I could never forget.

Our horses trot up to the Dais's house and stop. Yonah sighs happily and looks over at me. I look away at the house with orange light spilling from the windows.

"Dontaye," Yonah calls. I can't bring myself to face him, but he gently turns my face to him. I keep my eyes closed until I feel weightless when his lips touch mine. An ocean of tears wants to break the barriers I've set, but I won't let them. I want to enjoy this moment with Yonah for what it is. Not a goodbye forever, but a kiss. A kiss between a Guardian and his Belle because they've fallen in love.

When Yonah pulls away, I lean closer and find his lips again. He doesn't protest. He pulls me close and holds me tight. And then I feel it… the frown tugging at his lips, his kiss becoming more unraveled than before. Emotions he'd been holding back spilling from his mouth. There are things we've wanted to say to each other, but just couldn't find the words.

Yonah pulls away again but only to bury his face into the crook of my neck. He doesn't kiss it. He just breathes heavily against it, because he's fighting his own sadness. The consuming sadness.

Yonah stays in my arms until he slowly rises. His eyes avoid mine for a second before they lift to lock with mine. For once, the eyes of the Guardian hold no mystery to them. Pure sadness is all that is in them.

"Dontaye," he starts, "I—"

The front door opens and the orange light and sweet smell of honey and cinnamon whisk out on the chilly breeze.

"Dontaye's home!" Winter screams. She runs out onto the front porch in a winter white dress and snow boots.

"Winter," I call. Immediately jolting to my feet, I trip from the cart to swoop Winter up as she jogs through the snow. "Winter! It's freezing out here!"

"But," she says shyly, "you're finally home." Big blue eyes blink at me, and I feel my heart breaking.

"Oh, Winter," I whisper as I pull her into my chest. She squeals happily in my ear, and her brother appears in the doorway. He's wearing blue pajamas and standing in his boots. I extend a hand to him, and he races from the house, down the stairs, and through the snow to me. He plunges into us, but we make room for him.

With a twin clinging to either side of me, and Charlie and Rachel standing at the door, my heart swells with joy. This is my family who welcomed me home. I don't remember the last

182

time anyone welcomed me home, but this bittersweet moment makes me realize it's been a long time in my waking life since I had a real family.

With the twins, I stand to my feet holding each of their hands. Charlie comes out and kisses the top of my head before passing me to grab my bags. I look back once more to see the Guardian. He passes Charlie my bags and looks right over at me. To the naked eye, he's just a man. To the eyes of The Native, he's just the Guardian. But to me, Yonah is the one I love the most. And when I look back at him, I know he feels it, too. He doesn't wait for a goodbye; he simply inclines his head and yanks on the reins of the horses.

I walk with the twins to the door and Rachel opens her thick arms to welcome me.

"I'm … I'm home," I say shakily.

Rachel offers me her darling smile and says warmly, "Welcome home, sweet pea."

17

Dontaye

Though the night has been bitter with freezing air sapping the heat out of the flames, none of that seems to matter once Christmas morning arrives. Winter wakes me, jumping on my bed and screeching Christmas joy at the top of her lungs. I shove a pillow over my face to try to drown out her squeals so early in the morning. She climbs off me and races through the house to find her parents and wake them, too.

I roll over in bed and stare at the empty firepit. Stretching a hand out, I realize the flames died a while ago, but the joy of Christmas has kept us all warm. I smile to myself as I look at the empty pit. Today is Christmas, and for just today, I won't let the truth of my presence here in The Native weigh me down. I'll worry about that tomorrow, but today, I'll have fun.

"Dontaye?"

I look up from the pit to see Nite standing in matching

pajamas to his sister whose voice you can still hear singing somewhere in the house. "Merry Christmas."

I stand from the bed and cross the room to the doorway where Nite waits sleepily. "Merry Christmas, Aconite." I kneel and pull him in for a hug. He squeezes me tight before pulling away to tell me he's going to grab more wood to get started on the day before his parents get up. I leave him to it while I get freshened up and changed. Since it's Christmas, I'm going to give Rachel a break today and make her breakfast.

In the kitchen, I find her signature cast iron skillet, with all the scuffs and dents that certified her cooking as good. It's obviously the tool to use to nearly guarantee a perfectly good tasting meal. I throw strips of fresh bacon into the skillet, and then start on the grits when I hear Rachel's footsteps.

"Well, isn't this a merry Christmas?" She laughs heartily as she leans over and squeezes me into a hug. "I wasn't expecting to find you in the kitchen this morning."

"I'm sorry." I pour the milk into the grits until it seems right, then I glance up at her with a smile. "Were you planning something special?"

"Nothing too special. I was thinking of French toast today, along with pancakes."

"Lots of options," I say cheerfully.

She laughs. "I'll help."

Rachel grabs eggs and a porcelain blue bowl from the cabinet overhead. She only uses the expensive porcelain bowl Charlie bought her for Mother's Day two years ago for special occasions. Since I've been here, I've only heard about the bowl,

I've never actually seen Rachel use it until now.

"Today's Christmas," she offers with a smile and a hand on her plump hip, "the most special day of the year. We must use *the* bowl." She wiggles her fingers playfully at the bowl and I laugh.

We spend the morning together, swapping stories and telling each other secrets like we are old girlfriends or like actual mother and daughter. Of course, I didn't have much to tell since I couldn't remember much, but it was fun to hear all about how Rachel met Charlie at a church picnic when they were only nineteen. She said they were in love the moment they saw each other, and there was a bout of nostalgia that washed over me. It didn't threaten to send me into a haze, but instead, it made me feel warm inside, like there was someone I'd met and fallen in love with at first sight as well.

"After breakfast we'll head to the church for service, and then we'll spend the day making final alterations to our outfits for the night."

"Okay." I nod as I carry a plate of eggs to the table. Rachel explains that we don't exchange gifts. Having a healthy heart and a loving family is a really big gift. The only thing they ever want on Christmas is to go to The Native's festival. Everyone goes anyway, so it's all the buzz between the twins and Charlie, too.

Nite sits beside me as I hold Winter on my lap. We'll be

traveling only for a little while since our district is the closest to the center of The Native. From tall fir trees weighed down by fresh white snow, to flat land covered in a blanket of snow that reflects the golden light coming from the Nativity scene sitting in the center of a field—the entire Nativity was carved by our district, from the best wood we have to offer.

Mary and Joseph stand over baby Jesus as He lays in the manger smiling. The three kings and shepherds are kneeling and standing in the snow beside the lambs, and oxen, while the gifts from the three kings sit at the foot of the manger. There's an angel carved at the top of a wooden pole behind the entire Nativity scene, blowing a trumpet.

Our district worked hard to create the Nativity scene and make it as majestic as it was the day Jesus was born. Of course, this is only a replication, however, I think our display is beautiful. When I look at the scene, I can feel my eyes watering, and when I glance around the cart, there is silence. Even Winter and Nite are silent, looking on in awe. I catch Charlie wiping his eyes, but I choose not to make eye contact with him. Instead, I refocus on the Nativity and whisper a prayer of gratitude to God. A prayer of thankfulness that I get to experience Christmas in its rawest form—not an act of giving and getting, but a day of receiving from God.

The entire world received the presence of God the day Jesus was born. Peace On Earth literally lay in a manger, grew up, and walked the earth. The magnitude of Christ's birth shouldn't be limited to a single day of the year. When salvation was born, redemption was born. Joy was born. All of the goodness in the world was magnified by the birth of Christ, and He came with a never-ending supply of abundance and more. On Christmas Day, we received the revelation of God's love wrapped in flesh, and that is what should be celebrated and remembered.

After a time of reflection, our cart moves on and into the festival part of the celebration. The Native has completely transformed into a Christmas town. Black lamp poles reach for the sky and green garland hangs from each lamp, creating a chain of garland hanging above. Every pole holds a giant white candle that is wide and tall. They look like they'll burn forever. Beneath the lamp poles are all kinds of booths, songs, and dancing. The red booths are obviously from the Bleeding-Heart District. The purple booths are from Sugar Plum and the nutcrackers. And the tents where people eat, and commune are set up by the Ginger Folk. It's a beautiful atmosphere that I can't wait to enjoy.

We park our cart with a nutcracker who'll be in charge of feeding the horses. I feel bad that he doesn't get to enjoy all the festivities, but he says it's an honor to provide services in any matter during an event for Christ. That makes me feel a little better before whisking off with the twins clinging to either side of me. They begin dragging me along, and soon Charlie and Rachel disappear. I try looking back to find them, but they melt into the crowd and the twins aren't letting up.

"I want ice cream!" Winter exclaims. She and her brother are wearing matching outfits. Aconite wears crisp blue pants with a red sweater while Winter wears a red dress with a white turtleneck beneath it. She wears blue stockings to match her brother, and blue knockers in her big pigtails.

"Alright, we'll get ice cream." I nod, but Aconite starts pulling on my hand to whine, "I don't want ice cream. I want cookies!"

"We can get cookies, too," I try to sound convincing, but I'm only thinking of how I'll survive the night with these two.

"I want ice cream first," Winter says firmly.

"Okay, we'll get ice cream first, then cookies. Is that okay with both of you?"

"No," Aconite says, springing his hand free from mine. "I'm going to get cookies now!"

"Nite! Wait!" I call, but it doesn't even matter because Winter runs after him, and now I'm shoving through the crowd to catch these two. I'm losing them as I move through the blur of people. They're small, ducking and zipping by with no problems. I'm constantly issuing 'excuse mes' and apologies as I muscle my way through.

"If it isn't the Belle of The Native."

His voice stops me in my tracks, making me officially lose sight of the twins. Yonah steps out of the crowd, his heavy steps are loud even with the music and chatter of the entire Native going. He crushes the snow beneath his heavy boots and his wide shoulders move rhythmically as he approaches me.

"Yonah," I say softly. He brightens at his name as he pushes the loose dark hair from his face. I'll never get over his handsome face that always hides a little mystery in his eyes. The perfect jaw that was carved by God Himself. Bright eyes and a winning smile against his pale skin make Yonah hard to look away from.

"My Belle," he says as he kneels in the snow in front of the entire crowd and reaches for my hand. Mesmerized, I let him take it and kiss it. There are gasps through the crowd, but I choose to only focus on Yonah.

"Come," he says as he stands, "I need to take you somewhere before the night is over."

With my hand in his, we make our way through the watchful crowd. Every person we pass is gleaming with joy, waving kindly, and offering the season's greetings. It's a pleasant atmosphere. The dancing children from the Bleeding-Heart District, the caroling choirs from the Plum District, and the performers from the Ginger Folk who put on skits for crowds gathered under their tents. Every turn is something magical and colorful. I want to stay to enjoy the festival a little longer since it'd only begun, but Yonah is moving with a sense of urgency, so I follow without complaint.

He glances back at me once, offering a kind smile before guiding me ahead. I try to search for fear or worry in his quick glances, but my Guardian gives no wavering look. When we finally move through the crowd, we rustle through snow covered bushes until the festival behind us grows silent and The Native suddenly seems colder and darker.

"Where are we—"

"Shh," Yonah says quickly as he glances around. "Do you hear that?"

I squint into the chilly night, the outstretched darkness over the never-ending blanket of snow ahead of us. In the distance, I can hear a bell ringing.

"I hear a bell."

He smiles down at me. "Come on, that's what we're racing towards."

Swooping me into his arms, Yonah's heavy wings gush open. Shoving the air beneath his wings, we spring into the air smoothly, twisting through the frigid night until Yonah reaches a great height.

"Oh my goodness!" I scream giddily.

"This world is small compared to yours," he says as his wings flap in the air. The silver moonlight glows over us as Yonah holds me, suspended in the night's sky. The Native is even more beautiful than before. The love oozing from every surface of the land makes me want to leap from my Guardian's arms and let The Native embrace me as I fall.

"Belle," Yonah's voice is short and stern.

"Yes?"

"Thank you for being everything I'd hoped you would be. You have taught me much that I will cherish. And when we meet again, I'll be sure to remind you of our time together here. I'll tell you about all my adventures before you arrived, how they lacked the luster that a few days with you had."

I look out at The Native below in confusion and then back at him. "Why does this sound like goodbye?"

His eyes, for the first time since we've been floating before the moon, look away from mine.

"Yonah," I plead in a whisper. Bunching his sweater in my grasp, I plead again, "Yonah say something."

"It's time to go home, Belle."

I shake my head. "No. *No.* Things just got better. I want to be here! I don't want to go home! I want to stay here with Rachel and Charlie and the twins. I want to revisit all the districts. I... I..." I swallow thickly as I fight through tears to meet his sorrowful gaze. "I want to be with you, Yonah."

His smile is no longer bright, instead it looks broken as he presses his forehead against mine. "I wish things were different. But these are the plans of God. We are from two separate worlds, so we could never truly be together. Not here."

"We can make it somehow." Adjusting in his arms, I grab onto him with both hands. "Please, Yonah. Please don't do this."

"You have been the sweetness of The Native and the delight of my life. But now, I must return my Belle to the real world."

"Yonah—"

He silences me with a kiss. It's salty because my tears won't stop falling.

"Before the bell of The Native stops ringing, I must return you."

"I won't go." I begin to struggle against him. "I won't go! I won't go!"

Yonah holds me close as I break into a screaming fight, begging him not to take me. The warmth of his embrace makes me tired for some reason. It's like the more I fight, the sleepier I become. But even when I stop fighting and rest in his arms, I can't stop my eyes from closing.

"Please," I whisper once more.

"Until we meet again, my Belle, goodnight and Merry Christmas."

18

Ezra

My eyes feel heavy as I sit behind the wheel. I check my phone again to see if Dontaye's called, but there's nothing from her. There hasn't been anything from her and I'm getting worried.

I sigh as I squeeze the steering wheel. I can feel the heated leather beneath my palms, it's enough to make them sweat, so I release the wheel and turn off the heat. Immediately, I feel a chill inch up my spine. The weather has changed dramatically. Blue skies are a memory hidden behind the grey clouds that release tears of snow. I wonder absently if the snow will make Dontaye's return troubling. I don't know why she would go to Japan now anyway.

I don't know why she does any of the things she does. I blink out at the snowy road as I cruise to my place. The black top is still visible on some parts of the road, while others have a thin blanket of snow resting over it.

The snow... Taye hates the snow, I say to myself. More than usual, Taye's been on my mind. I've always cared for her because no one else has ever cared. I remember befriending her in college and eventually finding out her dark secret—that she hated God and her mother. Taye's just lost, that's what I've always told myself to feel better about hanging on to her. She's an assignment, someone I have to keep praying for... but in reality, do I really? In reality, I never really had to. I just *wanted* to. There was something about Taye that I liked immediately. It was probably just a crush, but I was too stubborn to let her go, and now it's turned into something that neither of us has words to explain.

Everyone knows friends of the world are enemies to God, no matter what you say or how you try to fix it. We can't fix what isn't broken. The Bible is very clear, there's no adjustments needed, yet I find myself hoping that maybe I've read the text wrong. Hoping there's a way around what's been instructed, but I know there isn't. There's no way around any instruction the Bible gives, but we let our human nature try to explain away the things we have no self-discipline for.

I pull into the parking lot of my apartment and just sit there staring ahead. I stare at the tall, black, and square building. It looks like someone stacked black painted shipping containers atop one another and shoved windows into random places in the metal frames. With a sigh, I lean back into my seat, feeling the weight of sudden exhaustion pressing down on me.

"Why do I feel so—"

My words are cut off when a raven drops out of nowhere onto the hood of my car. The thud is loud, like the raven is actually the weight of a grown man hitting the car. And then it begins to call loudly, right at me. It's glistening black body heaves deeply to shout at me. The raven stares through the windshield, cawing and squawking. I don't know what to do, except look right back at it in disbelief. I don't even know if ravens are native to this area, and even if they are, this one literally dropped out of nowhere. Its beady eyes hold something that isn't normal in them. They hold emotion... more emotion than a normal raven should have.

I must be sick; I tell myself as I feel my head. I close my eyes for a long moment, hoping this is just a crazy dream until I open my eyes, and find the raven still there.

What is going on?

It's quiet now, sitting on the hood, tilting its head to look at me. I look at the bird for a while, hoping that when I close my eyes this time, the bird will be gone, and this will all be something that never really happened.

I close my eyes and count to three. When I open them, the raven thrusts open its wings and leaps from the hood of my car. All that it leaves behind is a single feather stuck to my windshield. It takes me a second to move, but when I do, I throw my door open and run to the front of my car to check the hood.

"There's not even a scratch," I whisper as I lean forward and grab the feather. The moment I touch it, I feel my body go limp. I sag against the running car and drop to my knees.

The wet ground sends chills through my entire body and suddenly the world goes black.

A bright light burns my eyes as I open them. The light is warm and refreshing, tickling my frame as it washes over me. But there's something masked in the light, an uneasy feeling that begins to suffocate me... literally. I feel my throat closing and it jolts me up. I lunge forward, clutching my throat, gasping for air. *What's wrong with me? What's happening?* Somehow, the place I'm in causes me to feel even more suffocated. There are no tight walls to lock me in, or ropes to strap me to a chair. I'm just here, in a place between light and darkness, where nothing exists, nothing happens.

"I wouldn't say *nothing* is happening," says a voice that sounds eerily similar to mine. I glance around, searching for the voice, still clutching my throat. "Don't worry," the voice says, "you can breathe, you just didn't know it."

Shakily, I let go of my throat and realize I am breathing. I cough a little, but mostly out of embarrassment.

"Stand up," the voice says, and I only listen because there's no one else here and that voice just saved me. The sound of thick boots thudding through the empty place echoes and vibrates right through me. From the darkness into the light, I see a man step forward and I gasp because this man looks exactly like me.

"Shocked?" he asks, offering a gentle smile. "I've wanted to meet you." When he pauses, his smile sinks into a frown. "I ... I wish that I could be you. You just don't know how good you have it."

"You… you are—"

"I'm a version of you." He steps closer. "Soon, we'll be one, and you'll feel everything I've been feeling."

When he glances off, I take him in. I don't know what version of me this person claims to be, but I'm glad he's me. He's handsome and beautiful. He's like the perfected version of me, a version of me I've only seen in my dreams.

"I brought you here," he interrupts the silence and calls my attention back to him. "This realm between consciousness and unconsciousness. You needed to be conscious enough to accept me, but unconscious enough to forget. What happens outside of time cannot affect what happens in real time for *her* sake. If things change too much, she'll change with them."

I squint and find my voice, "Who will change?"

He smiles and it's warm and contagious. I feel my own cheeks pulling into a smile, with a rush of emotions twisting in my belly.

"We're already merging," he says, "you're smiling because I'm smiling, and what you're feeling is what I'm feeling." He takes another step closer, and I can feel something change within me in response. His presence is all around me yet pushing its way inside me.

"What's happening?"

"Time is ticking," he says, "and every step I take brings us closer together."

I shake my head. "I don't understand any of this. What's going on? Who are you?"

"I'm Yonah, Guardian of The Native. A version of you,

Ezra. The part of you that has always looked after her."

For a second, I almost know who he is talking about, but the face never comes, and the name dies on my lips before I can speak.

"You'll remember once we're completely merged. I'm just giving the others time to explain themselves to their counterparts. To the real them." He pauses. "Unfortunately, we're only a portion of each of you. And we must return to ourselves. For your sake and hers. If we don't return, each human will be missing a part of themselves they can never get back. It'll be lost forever, ceasing to exist."

I still don't understand, but Yonah understands this and waves a hand out beside us. I turn to see what looks like a movie playing beside me and Yonah begins to narrate, "We'll cease to exist if we don't reconnect with humanity. We make up parts of you, versions of you, perfected parts of you. Reconnecting allows us to continue living. Like this family," he says as he points to a woman with red hair and two small children, "they're Ginger Folk, and they're going back to the little shop they own in Japan. Everyone comes to see them, people from all walks of life." He looks over at me. "They were nomads in The Native."

"I don't know if I understand what I'm looking at."

Yonah bobs his head. "It may be a lot to take in all at once, but the importance of this is seeing how each of these people impacted her."

"Who's this woman you're always speaking of?"

Yonah doesn't answer my question, he just waves a hand

and a new image appears. There's another red-headed woman standing in front of a fireplace with stockings hanging on it. "She was merely an airplane passenger, but it was the book in her hands that stirred the girl's heart." He waves again and a castle comes into view, with a horde of people as white as snow standing in front of it. The entire image is bleak, except for the explosion of color coming from the fairytale creature standing in front, with a line of nutcrackers standing on either side of her.

"What is this?"

"It's a district she went to. Colorless, this place represented bad situations that took all the excitement from her life. And the people here were all people who hurt her in reality."

I look at the picture a little longer and a pang of guilt begins to eat away at me. "Why does the fairytale woman make me feel this way?"

"She's a fairy," he explains, "and it's our guilt. We never loved her, though she loved us."

"Who is she?"

"She was," he pauses to find the right words, "a woman I pretended to love while waiting for Belle. She would've been a wonderful woman. She would've been more loyal if I had loved her properly. But she knew as much as I did that someone else had my heart, no matter how much I pretended."

I can feel my cheeks burning with embarrassment. Though my memory is blocked, I know that Yonah is reciting something that happened to me. He's retelling a story of my own love—or pretend love—and a woman I ended up hurting because of that.

"Lastly," he brings up a family sitting together. Twin children that look so much alike I can't tell if they're two little girls or a little boy and girl, but the family looks happy. Sitting around a table, smiling at one another. "This is the Dais family. They have no one to return to, but they will continue to serve a purpose in her life. They will be a memory she can't remember, but a feeling she'll never forget. She will always strive to recreate the warmth she felt from that family with strangers, friends, and even her own family."

For some reason, I feel a little emotional, but I try to ignore it until the Guardian version of me waves his hand to close the visions and takes another step closer. With the gap closed between us, there's a sudden change in my heart. It begins to swell with emotions. Running right to the brim with heartbreak and a desire to live.

He wants to see her, this mysterious girl, I realize. I can feel his love for her, but it blurs the lines of my own feelings for someone special. It's an identical feeling... it's a—

"Replica," he finishes for me. "What I feel is a replica of what you've kept inside all along." Yonah's smile eases into a frown again and I watch his shimmering eyes fill with tears. He hangs his head before any of the tears fall, dark bangs falling into his face, broad shoulders trembling, and the weight of his cloak bouncing with his shaking shoulders. "I wanted to spend eternity with her. I wanted to stay," he whispers. "I wanted to love her, *me,* this version." He looks up with a gloved hand to his chest. Tears roll down his glowing cheeks, and as I look him over, I realize he's fading.

He sniffles and says, "The time has come." He reaches out his hand and grabs mine. His touch is so gentle, it's almost as if I grabbed the hand of a shadow. Interlocking his fingers with mine, he says, "I will be watching, so please take care of her for me."

I swallow, feeling the weight of all his emotions pouring into my chest. My eyes burn with tears, and I find myself nodding and promising, "I will. I'll look after her."

"Thank you, Ezra."

I begin to sob as Yonah fades right in front of me. The feeling of disappearing was something that could not be compared to anything I've ever felt. It was a blur of emotions, the kind that comes from a neatly painted portrait getting a water spill, and all of your favorite colors begin to bleed into one another. What was once a painting to admire, is now a confusing mess of colors, not even one particular color is distinct. It's all just a mess of them together, covering the masterpiece that once was. The picture will never be the same again, the portrait is lost, and now something else is being portrayed. But I guess that's what he meant when he asked me to look after this girl. The original masterpiece has changed now, bringing everything together. It's my job to try to continue to portray what the masterpiece sought to do initially.

Can I live up to Yonah's expectations? Will I make him proud? Somehow while living through me, will he be able to feel the wholeness he wanted?

"Yonah," I whisper in a shaky voice as I wipe my tears... his tears, "I'll do it. I promise I will." I swallow hard, trying to ignore the silence. He can't answer me anymore, but he can feel what I feel, see the things that I see. I place a hand on my chest and take a deep breath.

In the empty place where Yonah once was, a feather floats down. It eases through the air of this emptiness, dancing back and forth as it reaches the ground. I stretch out my hand to touch it, and when I do, a shock of electricity zips through me and light consumes me.

I sit up quickly and glance around. My car is still running, and the snow has begun to fall. My clothes aren't soaked, but I'm cold. I wasn't out for long, but I don't remember anything after the crow... raven? I rub a hand through my hair before standing. I hear my phone slip from my pocket, and as I turn to grab it, I see a feather sitting beside it.

"Yon—"

I stop. I almost remember something important, but it's overshadowed by an urge to call Dontaye. No memory or anything feels as important as making this phone call. I reach down and snatch up my phone to call Dontaye as I stare at the feather, wondering why it's making me feel so broken yet so complete.

19

Dontaye

I jerk awake, panting hard and glancing around as I sit up. My phone is sitting beside me, ringing loudly. The light from my phone blares brightly as it continues to ring. I squint, my blurring vision finally clearing, and read the name on the phone: Ezra. Snatching the phone up, I remember I told him to call me if he didn't hear from me.

"Hello?" my voice comes out in a shocking rasp.

"Dontaye? What took you so long to answer?"

I shove a hand to my head. "I ... I was asleep. I think."

"What? Where are you?"

I try to figure out where I am. "I think I'm in a cave."

"A cave?"

Ezra's voice falls to the back of my mind as I move to get up. Squeezing the phone to my ear, I absently listen to his complaints about my safety as I look around the cave. There's a little shrine before me, where a silver goblet sits empty.

"I remember," I say over Ezra's chatter. "I came here with some people who told me about a hidden shrine. They said there was ancient wine here."

"Please don't tell me you drank the wine?" he complains.

"And ate the bread that was here." I pause. "And that's when I passed out."

"Thank God all you did was pass out from *ancient* wine and bread, Dontaye! You need to get to a hospital and see—"

"It was communion," I whisper as I kneel and pick up the silver cup. The shrine ahead of me doesn't look like any other ancient Japanese shrine. I've seen a few, but this looks different. Not to mention that usually these shrines are not inside of caves. There's something like an altar with golden candles burning on it. There's a white sheet over the altar and an empty silver platter, obviously where the communion was.

"I've never heard of someone taking communion and passing out in a cave, Dontaye."

I stare at the empty silver platter, forcing myself to focus on what the man told me communion represents. "The body and blood of Jesus, it's a representation of Jesus' sacrifice on the cross. His life ending so ours can begin." I heave a deep sigh into the phone as realization strikes me. "My second chance. That's what I dreamed about." My eyes began to fill with tears as the memories come swarming back. Yonah, Rachel, the twins, and Charlie. All the districts and even all the monsters Yonah defeated. "And Jesus…" I gasp as my tears fell. "He showed up, too. He showed me that I always had a choice. He showed me that I could forgive and move on." I sniffle loudly. "This is my second chance, Ezra."

"Okay," he says calmly on the other end. "Calm down, Dontaye. You're saying a lot of stuff, and I don't really know if you understand—"

"I came on this trip to prove that religion should be eradicated from the world, but I was wrong. I was so wrong." I drop to my knees and begin to sob. "I was so wrong!" My chest feels tighter with every breath. I can hear Ezra trying to calm me down but there's a war within me. The overwhelming feelings of relief and remorse for my past is fighting for dominance in my heart.

"Dontaye," Ezra's voice reminds me of my Guardian's voice. Resolute and completely calm, like my very name from his lips can summon a silence to my storm. "Listen to me. I want you to come home. I know you still have some time left on your trip, but I seriously think you should consider returning early."

"You don't believe me." I shake my head. "Ezra, you're the person who *should* believe me, but you don't."

"I want to believe you, but I don't understand this."

"This *what?*"

"This sudden change."

I pause. "My conversion? Weren't you always the one telling me that God could make a sinner a saint in one breath? You used to tell me that in college. So why is this so hard to believe?"

"Because you were knocked out, Dontaye. That's not

normal."

"Well, God works in mysterious ways, or so everyone says." I stand and swipe at my tears. Feeling along the cave wall, I follow the trail to find the exit.

"Dontaye—"

"I'll call you later, Ezra. I need to figure this out on my own."

"Dontaye, please, I'm just trying to understand."

"I know. Me too. Which is why I need to do this alone."

I hang up the phone without waiting for his response. I understand his confusion. I understand it more than he thinks I do. He wants this to be real, not me bumping my head and changing. But he doesn't know all the details, so I can't be angry at him. I don't even have all the details yet; all I know is that I arrived at this cave, took communion, and fell asleep. The dream I had is already starting to fade. I'm clinging to the memories for dear life as I find my way out of the cave and into the mountain path.

I stop walking and stare at the sign for Rebirth Cave. A memory flickers in my mind of the old man who led me up here. He said that I'd be able to read the sign later. My throat tightens as I look at it. It's a small plank of wood on a stick jammed into the snow with the words carved into it and a bell hanging from the plank.

"Rebirth Cave, celebrate the birth of a new you." I run a hand over the sign. "The birth of a new you." There's another sign that names the path to the cave, "Canal." Like a birthing canal, and the actual cave is the place of rebirth. You're reborn in the cave, like a second chance. I feel my shoulders drop as every piece of the puzzle begins to fit into place.

Being reborn in the cave is a second chance, your new life, after acknowledging the life of Jesus through communion. And walking the path back home from the cave is like exiting the birth canal, the final part of your rebirth. You begin walking the path of righteousness. Of course, none of this made sense when I first arrived because I didn't believe, and I was looking at it backwards. Thinking this path *only* led to your rebirth, never realizing it is also the path to follow once you were reborn.

"Celebrate the birth of a new you." I shake my head as a small chuckle escapes me. "The birth of a new you—the birth of *anything* is called a nativity." I croak at the realization, feeling instant nostalgia as the name slips from my lips, "The Native." That's the dream land that took me back to my origins, where my rebirth needed to happen. The place where I accepted a second chance. The word native means origin, and that's exactly where I went, back to the origin of all my pain and hurt, just to be reborn. But there was more to it.

I sigh as I take the bell in my hand. When I came up the mountain, the people told me I could only ring it once I came out of the cave. It was symbolic of life ending and beginning again, like a timer stopping and starting all at once...

"That was me," I say aloud. "I was the bell. I was the bell of The Native, ringing to end their life but to begin mine."

Whipping open my phone, I begin jotting everything down in a note. I start with the dream and write down the parts of it I can remember. Then I finish with the cave and all it means for me and who I was as the bell, and as his belle. A tear plops onto the phone screen as all the emotions fill me. I reach to wipe it when my phone starts ringing. It's Ezra… again.

"Hello?"

"Taye, I'm sorry I overreacted. I was just confused and scared that something might've been wrong. I don't know, Taye, I'm sorry."

I nod, though he can't see me. "I'm going to come home early," I say. "I think this trip is over for me." I stop to pull the phone away and swap screens to my notes. I skim through them before returning the phone to my ear. "I have something I need to tell you. Will you listen to me?"

"I promise I will, just come home in one piece."

I laugh lightly. "I will."

"Then I'll be there waiting for you when you return."

My ears begin to burn, and a nervous heat swirls in my chest. "Don't be late." I try not to sound emotional.

His gentle laugh sooths my nerves as he says, "I'll be there. Don't worry."

20

Dontaye

Despite writing down the parts of the dream I could remember, whenever I reread it, it sounds like some story I've made up. I have nearly no recollection of the dream, but I understand everything I wrote down. It all makes so much sense to me, even though I can't imagine living through any of this, it's like reading the solution to a math problem while also looking at the equation. You didn't figure out the solution, but when it's there beside the problem, it makes sense that this result is the outcome.

I was a wreck before the dreamland. I was bitter and angry, overflowing with resentment towards everyone, especially God and my mother. Despite my anger, God's love still chased me down. He never stopped giving me opportunities to repent and receive His salvation and peace. He never stopped doing things to get my attention, even when I ignored Him. The love of a father is relentless. Even for one of the most stubborn people on earth, He never stopped pouring out His love. Every day was another chance to receive Him. God doesn't stop reaching for us until the very end.

God had a plan to reach me, right from the start of my life. An elaborate dream that would take me through a world where faith and total dependence on God would get even the most broken people through everything they faced. I had to relearn who God was through those districts. I had to encounter the faith of those who lived in The Native to understand that bad circumstances and problems don't stop you from living. You keep going to get to the good. To get to the promised relief, whether that be a child born to be king, or a Mouse King caught in a trap. Your second chance is coming, your new life will begin.

Each district represented a part of me. The Forestry District was my origin. That was where I learned to stop being selfish. It was the place that broke down my pride and all my walls. Seeing a family working together and accepting me ended up breaking me, even though I didn't believe like them and had wished to leave. That place planted a new seed of hope within me. God used the familial ties of the Forestry District to remind me that I was still loved, no matter the bad decisions or mistakes that I'd made. That district reminded me that I couldn't run away because there was a family of Believers waiting with open arms for my return. *God* was waiting with open arms.

The Bleeding-Heart District was my unbelief, showing me

that God would still love me though I didn't believe in Him. He would fight an entire army just for me, even though I should have been cast away to the darkness I wanted.

The Plum District was my mindset. I was broken and let all the anger and bitterness eat away at the little bit of happiness I did have, blotting out the color of my life. Yet God was willing to restore my joy and make my life even better than before.

And how could I forget the Ginger Folk, the nomadic people that kept believing despite their unwavering troubles. They were literally on the move and had no relief from the fox who chased them. Their problems hemmed at their heels, but they never stopped. They were constantly moving, but they adjusted their lifestyle and kept serving God. And He brought them to a land of peace. He brought them out of their silent fear to a loud and vibrant community. They were my future. The promise that no matter how far I ran, God was going to deliver me.

So, what reason did I still have to not believe in God? God delivered the Gingers, rescued the Plums, saved the Hearts, and gave warmth to the Forest. Four sides of God were shown to me… four sides of Jesus Christ. He is a rescuer, a savior, a deliverer, a restorer. Jesus died so that I can have all these things again. Even though I thought I'd lost everything, I hadn't. My life was only beginning through the pain. God always had a plan for me, I just couldn't see it. But now my eyes were open, and I could see clearly.

The only question left in my mind were the last words of

my Guardian before I woke up. He told me that he and I could never be together because we weren't from the same world. He loved me and longed to be with me, but two people from two different worlds could never be yoked together. Initially, I thought we could never be together because he lived in my dreams, but I realized that he was speaking metaphorically.

Love is a choice and a development. It is the essence of choosing to continue the journey with someone despite the blips and faults that may arise. It is the development of a union, where two people find that, against all odds, the longer they stay together, the stronger they become. A choice and development... that's why unequally yoked unions do not work out. Someone who is not in the same realm as you cannot choose to continue the journey with you because you both are traveling in two different ways. They cannot develop with you because the two of you are not impacting each other to cause development. You're incapable of impacting the inky shadows that dance along the walls when the light turns on.

While the light may expose the shadows, it doesn't make them go away. Don't get me wrong, the Light of Christ always puts the darkness to flight, however, darkness will always lurk. Temptation, sin, ungodliness, all of them are always watching from a distance, hoping for a chance to enter or reenter your life. A child of darkness will always be bound to the things of this world, and a child of Light will always be free to serve Christ. A free man cannot be impacted by the chains of a slave. He may feel pity, but he is unable to follow the same path of a slave, because a slave can only go as far as the chain will let them. Those who are bound to the world are unable to love. They cannot make that choice because they are bound to lust, the perverted and fragmented version of love.

I was no different. While Yonah only meant that we couldn't be together because he was going to become a memory when I awakened, the true meaning behind his words crushed me when I returned home. While I was on the flight, while I packed my things, while I waited in the airport, Yonah's words rang through me, though his face began to fade. But when I gathered my bags and stepped into the blizzarding world of Colorado, his words became so clear and palpable. I could literally see what he meant.

Standing by his car was the one guy that had always been there for me, and I knew would always be there. It was why he was my Guardian in The Native. It was why I loved Yonah with no explanation, because I'd loved him all along. But until I dreamed of The Native, he and I were part of two different worlds. I was a child of the dark, bound by the passions of this world, while the man I loved was a free man of Light. Our paths may have collided, but they never would've continued down the same way, not in the way of love... until now. Until I became free in Christ and became part of his world.

I stop, clutching to the handle of my bag as I blink at him. Amber eyes that are always brooding with something hidden in them seem to only swirl with fear and relief today. As tall and as mighty as my Guardian, even in his black puffer coat, and dark jeans tucked into mahogany brown boots, Ezra Friedman stands there waiting for me, like he never left.

"Ezra," my voice is barely audible as he rushes to me. Crushing me in his embrace, I realize that every embrace I had with Yonah was only a replica of this. Strong arms tightly wrap around me, holding my small frame to his large one as he whispers into my hair, "You're safe. You're home."

"Is this real?" I sniffle. "Are you here? I'm not dreaming?"

"You're wide awake," he says, rubbing circles into my back. "I'm right here, Dontaye." He steps back and lifts my hand to press it to his cheek. "I'm right here."

My eyes burn with tears, but I don't want my makeup running, so I fight hard to make sure they don't fall. "I'm home," I whisper.

"Welcome back."

Epilogue

1.5yrs later

I never wanted to admit that I'd always loved Dontaye. Since the day I met her, I have loved her. She was shy and quiet then with eyes that always looked defeated, like she'd given up before she'd ever given anything a try. Our general studies class together during our freshman year of college was one of the best classes of college. Because I'd met the love of my life in that class and was hoping that someday she'd realize she loved me, too.

It took a while to get from college to today, our very first Christmas together as a married couple, but the adventure was worth it.

"Merry Christmas, Dontaye," I whisper as she lay asleep on the couch. We spent the day exchanging gifts and eating all the boxed stuffing we could take, and then singing Christmas karaoke until our voices went hoarse. It was an eventful day for us.

I smile to myself as I sit on the wide leather chair of our apartment. It's fixed right in front of the Christmas tree that blares with flashing white lights twisted among the green branches. There's a quiet hum coming from the window lights that normally sing, but we turned the music off as the night wound down. So, I sit still and blink at the Christmas tree, reflecting on my first year of marriage with Dontaye.

She ended up changing her dissertation at the last minute. She argued that the world would *not* be better without religion, and she tied in the examples from her dream world. She compared them to the real world and the way of life from the cultures she'd studied.

I was proud to stand by her when she graduated as a doctor three days before our wedding. Dontaye was a beautiful bride. Her evenly toned brown skin seemed to glow against her winter white dress. Obviously, the theme of our wedding was tied to her dream. It was a wedding in The Native. One that'd been long awaited since the dream land was created.

I had to dress like her Guardian. She said she couldn't remember much about him now, but she remembered his cloak. It was heavy and weighed down with material that transformed into the feathers of his wings. She said he was the one she'd loved, and he loved her, and she was keeping the promise she'd made to reunite with her Guardian in the real world. I was almost upset about it until she said something I'll never forget.

"All along, I'd had fragmented memories while in The

Native," she'd said, looking out the window. We were shopping for an apartment together before our wedding, and she stood in the big floor-to-ceiling windows with a palm pressed against one. Brown curls rolled down her back, and her slender frame looked small against the wide window. "But all the memories that came back always involved one person. They all revolved around the mysterious person I truly loved. The one who was The Guardian of The Native because he was my guardian in real life."

She turned to face me, a smile on her face, her eyes sparkling like I'd never seen before. "The Guardian of The Native told me that I'd forget most things from that dream, but he'd also said while I was in The Native that I'd have the most trouble remembering the people I loved the most." She shrugged, glancing away from me to watch the snow fall again.

I stepped closer to her without even thinking, eager to finally know more about the mysteries of The Native. Dontaye didn't talk much about her dream, but all the stories were filled with something intriguing or some life lesson. I didn't particularly like that my future wife wanted to recreate a dream because she'd fallen in love in her sleep, but it was this day that I realized my beautiful fiancée had indeed fallen in love while she was *awake*.

"My Guardian," she started again, "he's the hardest to remember now. But I don't need to remember him because The Guardian of The Native was you, Ezra."

My heart had swelled in that moment, filled with complete joy. Ever since then, there's been times when I wondered if maybe The Native had been reality, and this beautiful, perfect love had become our dream. But I have this memory, or this image in my head of the Guardian my wife so loved. I often forget, but sometimes the memory is triggered by things she says. Things she does, and I choose to believe that in those moments, when I remember him, it's because he's reacting to his Belle, my wife, Dontaye.

I never told Taye that I met Yonah, mostly because I remember him randomly. Every time I think of him, it's bittersweet; but at the very least, I've stuck to my promise, and I plan to keep sticking to it.

"I promise," I whisper as I watch our Christmas tree blink with flashing lights. And even though Yonah isn't standing here, I can hear his words in my heart.

"Thank you, Ezra."

More books by A. BEAN & TRC Publishing!

Christian Fantasy

The Scribe

Cross Academy

Christian Post-Apocalyptic Fiction

The Barren Fields

The End of the World series

MAGOG saga

Christian Science Fiction

I AM MAN series

Christian Romance

The Living Water

Withered Rose Trilogy

Beautiful Lies

The Gap

Decipis Trilogy

Fractured Diamond

The Woof Pack Trilogy

Singlehood

Christian Children's Fiction

Too Young

ACKNOWLEDGEMENTS

For my mother, because I didn't want the grandkids to hear someone else's story the night before Christmas

Jesus is the Christ, Son of the Living God

God gave me this idea and I am grateful that we saw it through until the end together.

Valicity, hopefully I can write something else that'll impress you as much as this one did.

Thank you to you, the reader, for going on this Christmas adventure with me. I hope you'll check out some of my other work and find there's an adventure waiting for you there, too. Traveling through The Native was quite a journey, wasn't it? Let's go on another.

Follow me on **Amazon** and **Instagram** [@awritingbean] to get updates on new releases, pre-orders, and reduced prices on my books.

The Rebel Christian Publishing

We are an independent Christian publishing company focused on fantasy, science fiction, and romantic reads. Visit therebelchristian.com to check out our books or click the titles below!

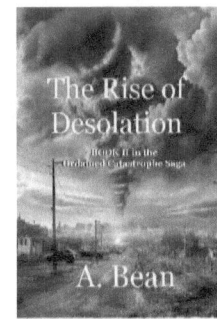
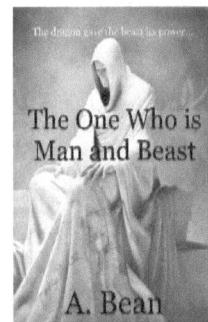

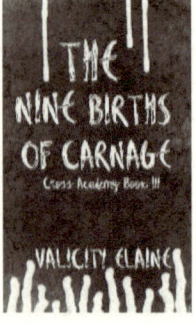

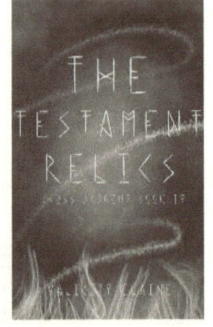

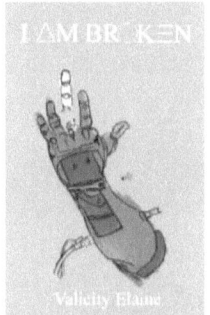

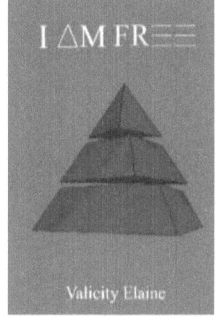

I △M
C_MPL_T_

Valicity Elaine

PATCHES

Valicity
Elaine

The I Word

Valicity Elaine